I only said leave me out of it

Dr. Celia Banting

WIGHITA PRESS

Wighita Press
P.O. Box 30399
Little Rock, Arkansas 72260-0399

www.wighitapress.com

This is a work of fiction. Names of characters, places, and incidents are products of the author's imagination and are used fictitiously and are not to be construed as real. Any resemblance to actual events, locales, organizations, or persons, living or dead, is purely coincidental.

Library of Congress Cataloging-in-Publication Data

Banting, Celia
I Only Said Leave Me Out Of It/Dr. Celia Banting – 1st Edition
p. cm.
ISBN 9780978664893 (paperback)

1. Therapeutic novel   2. Suicide prevention   3. Divorce
4. Blended families

Library of Congress Control Number: 2007930370

Layout by Michelle VanGeest
Cover production by Luke Johnson

Printed by Dickinson Press, Grand Rapids, Michigan, USA

Issues addressed in this book:

Identical twins/nature versus nurture/effects on personality

Development of a conscience

Family scapegoats

Passive aggressiveness

Sarcasm

Bribery and manipulation

Co-dependency

Adultery/divorce

Abandonment

Coping with step-parents and step-siblings

Staying OK with injustice

Family therapy

Mind games versus true intimacy

Love versus being in love

Positive and negative Strokes

Karpman's Drama Triangle

Active listening skills

Ownership or rejection of step-parents/families

Dedicated to Erica Elsie. Also dedicated to Joe and Ann Daly, and all those who turn divorce and remarriage into a happy, blended family where everyone has a valued and special place .

Acknowledgments

My grateful thanks go to my proofreader and typesetter, Michelle VanGeest, who frees me from my dyslexic brain, and replaces my mother's voice. Thanks to Bev, my stray-word spotter, too. I thank my wonderful husband, Des, for the inspiration and support he gives me. Thank you to Luke and Sam for their faith, inspiration and talent. Thank you to Helen and Dave, and Moya and Tony for their faith and support. Thank you also to Susan Harring and Ron Woldyk for their reliability and professionalism. Thank you to my dear friend Vicki for her guiding sense of style.

Thank you to Dr. Claude Steiner for the great gift he has given humankind by explaining operant conditioning in terms of Warm Fuzzies and Cold Pricklies, which enables *everyone* to understand a complex concept in simple, accessible and amusing terms. Thank you, Dr. Steiner, for your analogy of one's "heart" being a Fuzzie Bag. Thank you to Stephen Karpman for his "Drama Triangle," which simplifies Dr. Eric Berne's concept of psychological game-playing.

Thank you to all my psychotherapy tutors and colleagues at the Metanoia Institute, London, for teaching me about human nature, psychopathology, growth and recovery.

I thank the good Lord for giving me a lively imagination, and I also thank my parents for moving to the Isle of Wight, "the land that bobs in and out of view, depending upon the sea mist."

Chapter One

"Whatever!" Lesley snarls at me.

"Will you two just stop it? I'm sick of you arguing," Mom shouts, as she hangs a shiny ornament on the Christmas tree.

"Well, Maizy started it," Lesley whines.

"Maizy, go to your room."

"Mom, that's not fair." I can feel tears prick my eyes as a sense of injustice swamps me. How come Lesley can twist everything around so that it's always my fault and I get into trouble?

"Don't argue with me. Go to your room!" Mom raises her voice.

Out of the corner of my eye, I see Lesley smirking. Something snaps inside me. No, I'm not going to my room again. It's always me that Mom sends away when Lesley and I fight. I'm going across the road to old Mrs. White's house to feed Sooty, her cat.

"What's all the noise about?" Dad asks, as he opens the front door.

"It's the twins again," Mom snaps. "Do something with them. I can't do everything on my own."

Lesley flops down on the sofa in front of the TV and acts all innocent while I tell my side of the story, praying that Dad will stick up for me. He lets me down.

"Maizy, just do as you're told, love. Go to your room," he says, with a plea on his face. I love my dad so much, but I wish he'd stand up for me just once.

Frustration flares inside me, and I refuse to be confined to my room because Lesley has gotten me in trouble yet again.

"I hate you, Lesley," I yell, but she laughs, turning around so that Mom can't see her as I grab my coat before slamming the door behind me.

I can still hear Mom yelling at Dad, blaming him for all the arguments in our house. What's wrong with them? Why can't they see that it's Lesley who makes all the trouble? She gets away with everything.

I trudge my way through the snow, across the deserted road, towards Mrs. White's house. I've been helping her for years now, since she had a stroke and lost the use of her right arm. At first Lesley and I used to take turns to go but after Lesley tried to tie a firecracker to Sooty's tail, Mrs. White told her to never come back. At first I resented having to do it all by myself, but as Lesley and I argued more and more I was glad to have somewhere to go where she couldn't follow me.

I can't believe that we're identical twins. Everything about us is the same, even down to the little black mole on our right cheeks, yet I think we're totally different inside. Lesley's mean and hateful, and I'm not. Okay, so I argue at times, but she drives me to it. Mom always takes her side and never listens to me. It's not fair. Sometimes I think Mom can't be bothered to sort out our fights and just sends me to my room because Lesley seems to be louder and sneakier than I am.

Thoughts flood my mind as I let myself into Mrs. White's house—she's gone to her daughter's for Christmas. Sooty runs up to me and weaves in and out of my legs, pleased to see me. I fill her dish with food and pour milk into her bowl before sitting in Mrs. White's rocking chair.

• • • •

Life at home has always been the same, for as long as I can remember. Even when we were really little, Lesley pushed me around. Mom used to tell everyone that I was the quiet one and Lesley was the leader. I always had second choice. It didn't matter what we were given, she always chose first and I had what was left over. Mom used to dress us the same but got so fed up with Lesley yelling that my clothes were hers that she finally dressed us differently so that there could be no arguments.

Whatever I had, Lesley wanted. When we were younger I gave in because, frankly, she scared me when she yelled and screamed, but that changed on our sixteenth birthday.

Although I'd tried to keep it a secret at home that I liked a guy at school, I guess Lesley and her friends heard rumors. My best friend, Judy, and I spent every break at school following Mark and his friends. When they ran track we sat and watched, and when they charged down the field at football practice we cheered loudly. He didn't seem to notice that I was alive even after Judy stuffed a note into his hand one day.

"What did you do?" I asked her.

"Nothing," she grinned. "Just helping out."

Every day was filled with thoughts of Mark, and I often got into trouble for daydreaming in class. I lived to see him in the halls when the bell rang and we pushed our way through the crowds to our next class. We didn't hang out with the other girls during break but positioned ourselves as close to him and his friends as possible without being too obvious. I guess I wasn't as subtle as I thought I was, because, although I didn't realize it at the time, my sister had obviously noticed.

It was the day of our birthday during lunch. I nearly died when Mark walked across the cafeteria towards me, smiled and said, "You're awesome." He just walked past and I could feel my face burning and my heart thumping. Judy dug me in the ribs and said, "Go girl."

Looking back I can barely remember the rest of the day because I floated around on cloud nine. He'd noticed me and thought I was awesome. Yeah!

Sooty breaks into my thoughts as she leaps up onto my lap and nestles down, purring with happiness. I rock in the chair, stroke the cat, and follow my thoughts.

Mom and Dad had planned to take us bowling for our birthday and said that we could bring a friend. Naturally I asked Judy to come along. I'd have rather celebrated my birthday separately, without Lesley, and without my parents, but I didn't object because I didn't want to upset Mom and Dad. Having Judy there would make it okay, or so I thought.

She came to my house after school to get ready, not that we bothered to dress up. We both wore jeans and a top. Judy and I sat in the back of the car watching Mom stand in the doorway yelling up the stairs, telling Lesley to hurry up. Judy nudged me in the ribs as Lesley appeared.

"She looks like a whore," she snickered in my ear, and sure enough when I looked at Lesley, I couldn't help but agree. She wore a miniskirt that covered nothing and a low-cut top that exposed everything.

"What're you looking at?" she demanded, as she sidled into the car next to Judy.

"Nothing," we said together.

I tried to stifle a giggle as Judy continued to dig me in the ribs.

"Nice skirt," she said to Lesley, and I could tell from her tone of voice that she was being sarcastic.

Lesley scowled and turned up her nose as she looked Judy up and down.

"Nice last-year jeans," she bit back, but Judy didn't seem upset. She nudged my ankle and I shrunk back into my seat. Judy had told me over and over to stand up for myself when my sister picked on me. Judy seemed stronger than me and I was glad she was there. She didn't care if she upset Lesley.

"Are you wearing a padded bra?" Judy asked, staring at Lesley's breasts that were fighting to escape her skimpy top.

Lesley gritted her teeth and mouthed the "B" word at Judy so that my parents wouldn't hear. Judy put a rude hand gesture in her face and my stomach turned over in a double flip. Happy birthday, Maizy!

I couldn't wait to get out of the car; luckily we didn't have far to go. Mom fussed with her purse as we all piled out. I was relieved to be away from the oppressive hatred in the back seat. I admired Judy for standing her ground against Lesley. It was something I'd never managed to do.

We'd been bowling for a while and Dad kept going on about our teams being unfair since Lesley's best friend hadn't showed up, which left her side one short. Mom asked her where she was, and Lesley kept glancing at her watch and at the door. I felt a strange sense of satisfaction that no one had bothered to turn up—perhaps her "friends" knew how mean she was. But then my thoughts crashed in on themselves as Lesley's face lit up. Mark! She ran towards the door and threw her arms around Mark. She kissed him hard before leading him by the hand towards Mom and Dad.

My mouth fell open and tears pricked my eyes. Judy was just as shocked. My heart was broken in two and I struggled to hide my feelings.

Dad shook Mark's hand and was goofy, trying to talk man to man with him.

"So, Mark, are you in the same class as Lesley?"

"No, sir. I'm in the year above her."

"Are you in the same clubs then?" Dad pressed. "I mean, how did you two meet?"

"No, we're not in the same clubs, but she likes to watch me run and play football. She's there every day," Mark said, as I swallowed hard, not believing what I was hearing. He was talking about me, not Lesley. "We got together a week ago. She's awesome."

When did they get together? What did she do? As I realized that she'd pretended to be me—so that's why he'd come over to me that day and said I was awesome—tears filled my eyes and I wiped them away, praying that no one saw.

"Yes, she *is* awesome," Dad beamed. "Both my girls are great."

Mark barely glanced at me and I looked away. His eyes were only for Lesley. She slipped her hand into his as Dad struggled to keep the conversation going, and all the time she had a gloating smirk on her face.

"D'you like my skirt?" she asked Mark loudly, keeping her gaze on Judy.

He almost choked and nodded fervently.

"What about my new top?" she said, rotating her shoulders and thrusting out her breasts.

Mark looked as if he was about to pass out. He nodded, "Yeah, um, very nice," he said thickly.

Lesley whispered into my ear. "Do you like my new boyfriend?" I felt such hatred rage through me that I didn't know what to do with my feelings. Judy started to flirt outrageously with Mark just to annoy Lesley. He looked confused but pleased, and Lesley cussed carefully at her when Mom and Dad weren't looking.

When we'd finished playing, Mom and Dad took us out to eat. I didn't want to go. I felt wooden, like a puppet, trying to control the pain I felt. They ordered everything, but I felt sick and just picked at my food. Lesley was obscene. She glanced at me to make sure that I was watching her and then she nudged Mark in the ribs, running her tongue over her ice cream, flashing her eyes seductively at him. He went very red and I don't know whether Mom and Dad noticed what she was doing. I did, and so did Judy.

Judy blurted into the conversation. "Um, Lesley, where's Jake? I thought you were going out with him."

Mark looked at Lesley, waiting for an answer, and if I hadn't felt so miserable, I'd have laughed at her discomfort. Lesley looked at Judy dangerously, and retorted, "I'm with Mark, can't you see?" She snuggled into him and he glanced awkwardly at Dad.

Judy didn't stop. "That's funny, because all the girls at school say you and Jake are together."

I watched Lesley grit her teeth. She was trying to control herself in front of Mark, who was looking at her, demanding an answer with his eyes. She was mad; I knew that look.

"You shouldn't listen to gossip," she said flippantly, tossing an icy stare at Judy, which she ignored. "Jake and I were over ages ago for your information," she snarled at Lesley.

"Oh really," Judy pressed, "I could've sworn I saw you kissing him two days ago at the end of soccer practice," she feigned innocence, and then she shrugged, saying, "Perhaps I got it wrong. Perhaps it was someone else." Then she shook her head deliberately and said, "No, it was you, I know it was."

There was a question on Mark's face, silent but demanding, and Dad glanced around the table sensing the awkwardness.

"So Judy, have you bowled before?" Dad said, his voice slightly higher than normal. "I thought you were going to beat us at one point. You're pretty good."

I recognized that voice—it was the one he used when trying to calm everyone down. Everyone looked at him.

Judy looked around the table, totally fearless, and said, "Not as good as Lesley. Perhaps she practices with Jake," she added, smiling at Lesley with contempt in her eyes.

Lesley floundered for a moment but then came back at Judy. "We won because of Mark," she said, staring into Judy's eyes, daring her to carry on. "Were you on the wrong side?" she asked.

Mom pushed her plate towards the center of the table, her jaw clenched, and I knew she was mad. "It's been a long day," she said, cutting across the raw animosity between Judy and Lesley. "Time to go, I think," she said, as she fumbled under the table to retrieve her purse.

Dad insisted that Mark should come back to our house. On the way home Judy hissed into my ear about standing up for myself and how evil my sister was to steal the guy I liked. She made an obscene hand gesture to Lesley as Dad dropped her off outside her house.

When we got home I got out of the car first. I couldn't bear to watch Lesley with Mark, and I wanted to rush to the sanctity of my room. I was so desperate to cry—to let out all my pain and anger.

Mom followed me up the path and said, "Maizy, put the kettle on and make some hot chocolate."

"No," I snapped. "I want to go to bed."

"Excuse me." Her voice had a dangerous edge to it—I'd crossed a line. "It may be your birthday but don't you sass me, young lady. Go and put the kettle on."

My jaw hurt as my teeth were clenched in anger and I tried to hide my feelings. Dad ushered Lesley and Mark through the front door and I disappeared into the kitchen, trying to get away from the gloating on Lesley's face. I felt consumed with rage and wanted to kill her. I hated how it made me feel, but I couldn't help it. I stood at the sink and took a deep breath, but Mom got on to me.

"What are you standing there for? Put the kettle on, will you?"

I snatched it up and turned the tap on as hard as I could, ignoring the water that sprayed over me.

"Maizy! Look what you're doing. Stop it. Look at the mess," she yelled.

I didn't care about the mess or being soaked by

spray. Nothing could make me feel any worse than I felt right then.

"What's gotten into you?" Mom nagged. "I only asked you to make some hot chocolate. Be nice. Lesley's brought her boyfriend home. What's wrong with you?"

Lesley poked her head around the door. "Mark likes two sugars," she said, laughing at me.

I couldn't help it, I cussed at her. Mom hissed into my face, "What's gotten into you? Why are you behaving this way? You're being rude. Stop it."

I gritted my teeth and made the hot chocolate. Mom told me to take the tray into the living room. She was mad so, because I didn't want to make her even angrier, I did what she said. She followed me with a plate of chocolate cookies.

"My sister's quite the little hot chocolate maker," Lesley taunted. "I'll take those, Mom," she said, reaching up to take the plate of cookies. She put them right beneath Mark's nose and said, "Hey, baby, have one. They are good."

I walked away, willing myself not to cry. I reached the stairs when Lesley, sensing she had lost her audience, jibed at me.

"Happy birthday, sissy. Perhaps next birthday you can bring *your* boyfriend."

I refused to face her or answer, but with anger distilling into rage, I walked up the stairs with as much dignity as I could.

I was glad that my room was first on the left because I barely made it through the door before collapsing on my bed, sobbing into my pillow as quietly as I could. I'd rather have died than show Lesley just how much she'd hurt me.

Later, I heard Mom and Dad go to bed and Mark leave, when a car pulled up outside our house and honked. I blew my nose when I heard Lesley coming up the stairs. The light beneath my door changed, casting shadows that told me she was outside my door. She didn't knock.

My door burst open and she stood there, proud, her face a triumph. She walked into my room and shut the door.

"It was *so* easy," she sneered. "D'you think you'd have gotten him by just watching and following him? You're pathetic. You don't know anything. All I had to do was mess around with him, promise him everything. He was all over me—couldn't get enough of me. He kisses like a dream," she jeered quietly so that she didn't alert Mom and Dad. "Did you really think that the most popular guy in school would fancy *you*? Give me a break. You're so lame—look at you."

Something snapped inside me and I leapt off my bed and flew at her. She screamed loudly and moments later Mom and Dad burst through my door.

"Arrrhh," Lesley cried dramatically, "she's trying to kill me. I didn't do anything."

Mom wrenched me away from Lesley, and Dad stood wringing his hands, looking wretched, not knowing what to do. Lesley was yelling, enjoying herself, and I was so mad that I couldn't stop from cussing at her.

"Stop it!" Mom shouted into my face. "What is *wrong* with you?"

I didn't get to answer before Lesley spoke out. "I only came into her room to wish her 'Happy Birthday' and she went crazy," she said innocently.

Mom pushed me towards my bed and yelled, "Get to bed," and with exasperation in her voice she yelled at Lesley, too. "I can't believe you girls. Why can't you get along? You're twins, for heaven sake. Get to bed, both of you. I've got to get up early."

She pushed Lesley out of my room and Dad followed silently. Lesley called out, "Good night, sissy. Happy birthday," as she went to her room, and I felt more hatred for her than I'd ever felt before. I felt consumed by it.

I lay on my bed, my heart racing. I felt so frustrated that I cried all over again and then punched my pillow and pretended it was Lesley, but that didn't help. I felt as if I was a mass of writhing feelings, like hissing snakes full of rage and venom. I didn't know what to do with myself, so I punched the wall and felt my knuckles crunch. The pain was better than the pain inside me. It shook me up and focused my senses away from the injustice I felt.

With my hand throbbing, I became calmer and laid on my bed, thinking. Every year Mom would take us to a twin convention, where hundreds of identical twins and their parents would meet. I hated it. I felt like an exhibit in a freak show. I felt worse when I saw how close the other twins were. It made me feel so alone and it made me question what was wrong with us. How could I look in the mirror and feel good about myself when all I saw was my hateful, vicious sister, exactly the same as me, even down to the mole on our cheeks? Did that mean that *I* was hateful, too? The thought that I could be like her sent a tide of pain surging through me, and a solitary tear spilled out of my eye and lodged in my ear. I had lain awake for hours.

Judy was fierce the next morning when I met her at school. She cussed Lesley out and told me that she'd fix it.

"Leave it," I cried. "It's no good."

She was mad and almost stamped her foot. "No, I won't leave it. Your sister's a..." She was very rude about her. "I'm going to let Mark know what she did."

"No, leave it," I begged. "You'll just make it worse. He didn't know I existed. Please, leave it."

But she wouldn't.

She pounced on him at break time. I hung back, praying that the ground would open up and swallow me whole, as she told him what Lesley had done. I felt more humiliated than I thought was possible when he laughed at her, and said, "Who cares? I want the one who gives me what I want."

Judy cussed him out and told him that he was a superficial jerk, and although I was grateful that she had stood up to him and fought in my corner, I felt worthless. It all felt messed up. Mark only wanted "me" if I behaved like a whore, which my sister had done impersonating me. I felt confused, angry and ashamed. What would he say in the locker room about me? Would all the boys at school now think that I was a whore and mistake me for Lesley?

"What a jerk!" Judy spat. "Your sister's welcome to him." She shook her head and slipped her arm through mine as she pulled me along the hall to our next class.

And that's how it was between my sister and I. She loathed me and I hated her, partly because I was scared of her vindictiveness—it was like she had no conscience. Yes, I knew I could be mean too, but I always felt bad about it later. She didn't.

She finished with Mark within days when she saw that I didn't care. Of course I still cared, but I learned to act as if I didn't and she got tired of baiting me. Mark told everyone at school how "easy" I was and the kids couldn't figure out which one of us was uptight and which one was a whore. The kids were mean and Judy got into lots of fights.

Fall turned into winter and a brittle truce resided in our house. Mom was busy, Dad took a new job and was out all the time, and Lesley was busy trying to win back her reputation while sabotaging mine. I worked hard at my grades and focused on Judy, who made me laugh all the time. I wished I were more like her. I studied hard and longed for the Christmas break. It finally arrived.

• • • •

Mrs. White's cat wakes up and stretches her legs, showing her claws, and she shakes me into the present. The anger I feel as my memories replay in my mind still bubbles inside me, but suddenly I feel sad. It's nearly Christmas and we're expecting Aunt Hettie and Grandma in a while. I love my Aunt Hettie—she's as loose as Mom is tight. I love Grandma, too. Since Grandpa died she's gone a little crazy.

I love Christmas and I don't want it to be ruined by my anger. I take a deep breath and decide to ignore Lesley. I gently push Sooty off my lap and refill her bowls again before slipping out of the door. I'm going to go across the road to our house and help Mom decorate the tree. Mom lets me help every year. I steel myself as I stomp through the snow determined to ignore Lesley's attempts to rile me and get me into trouble.

Chapter Two

Dad's in the yard chopping wood for the fire and he looks up as I pass him. He gives me a bleak smile and doesn't scold me for leaving the house. I give him a hug before letting myself back into the house.

Lesley's still sitting in front of the TV, warming her feet in front of the log fire. She glances my way and smirks. I feel the anger in my stomach uncurl like a stirring python, but I will it to back down. I focus on Mom who's leaning precariously across the Christmas tree trying to place more ornaments on the top branches.

"Can I help?" I ask, as brightly as I can.

She glances at me, and says, "Yes, hand me those glass balls."

Every year Mom decorates the house in red and green, and outside our house twinkles with thousands of lights as soon as the sun disappears. It's

Dad's job to keep the log fire going.

I pick up a box of red glass ornaments and hand her one.

"No, Maizy, not that one," Mom snaps. "Give me the red ball, no, not that one, *that* one."

They're all red, so I point to each of the glass balls, feeling stupid, until I reach the one she wants. Mom's panicking, I can tell. We're having a party this evening. I don't know why she bothers because she always gets so stressed when she invites people over. Perhaps once the tree is finished she'll calm down. I keep quiet, not wanting to antagonize her.

Dad comes through the door, his arms full of logs and his coat peppered with snowflakes.

Lesley calls out, "Hey, Dad, can we have some more logs on the fire?"

He piles up the logs next to the grate and Lesley dodges her head around him to watch a movie. My stomach churns as I watch her lying around on the sofa demanding more logs.

"What time are Grandma and Aunt Hettie coming?" Dad asks Mom, as she steps even higher on the ladder so that she can place the Christmas angel on top of the tree.

"I don't know," Mom snaps. "Any minute now, I guess. I hope they get here before everyone starts arriving."

Dad walks away, his shoulders slumped. I wish he'd stand up for himself when Mom picks on him, and I wish he'd stand up for me, too. Lesley pushes him around as much as Mom does, and he lets her. It makes me mad. Lesley twists him around her little finger and he gives her what she wants right away. He doesn't seem able to see what she's doing. He never stands up to her. I know I could get what I want from him, too, if I tried, but I don't want to do that. It's not fair.

"Hand me that box over there," Mom says to me and points to a box of glass icicles. "Be careful," she warns.

I hand them to her and she hangs them carefully around the tree. She climbs down the ladder and stands back to admire her work.

"It's beautiful, Mom," I say, meaning it.

"I'm hungry," Lesley calls over to us. "When's dinner?"

Mom frowns at her and says, "How can you be hungry? You've been snacking on popcorn. We'll eat when everyone gets here."

Lesley whines and mutters the last word under her breath. I can feel my jaw tense when I hear her being mean. My head spins as I try to control myself. It's so hard; I feel like every part of myself is tingling with animosity towards her.

Dad goes back to chopping more wood, and as I glance at him through the window, a car turns into the drive. The falling snowflakes dance in its head-lights.

"They're here," I cry, and my stomach does a double flip. I love my Aunt Hettie; she's so funny, and I know that having Grandma here will make Mom happy.

"Oh, no," Lesley sighs heavily, and mutters under her breath, "that means putting up with Grandma."

Mom doesn't seem to hear her and heads for the door. I follow her. When she opens the door I feel an icy blast of wind shoot into the house.

Dad puts down the axe and goes to help Aunt Hettie get Grandma out of the car. He puts his arm around her.

"Careful," Mom nags from the doorway. "She's already broken her hip once. I don't want her to fall."

Lesley stays in front of the television and complains about the icy wind making her neck cold.

Dad and Aunt Hettie struggle through the door, their arms around Grandma. Mom takes her coat and nags at Dad to bring in the rest of the bags from the car. His face is red from the cold.

Aunt Hettie stamps her feet on the mat to get rid of the loose snow and she takes off her coat. After she hugs Mom and me, she goes over to Lesley and plants a kiss on her cheek. Lesley ignores her and pulls a face as she rubs her cheek.

"How was the drive?" Mom asks.

"It was long—the roads are bad. I can't believe

that a drive which normally takes me half an hour took three times as long." Aunt Hettie whispers into Mom's ear, "And Mom had an accident, so the drive was kind of long and smelly."

Mom pulls a face, but then they both laugh. I watch the two of them together and wonder again why Lesley and I aren't close.

Dad struggles with their bags and I go to help him. He looks frozen. I love my dad so much, even if he doesn't stand up for himself or for me. He's kind and sweet and would do anything for anyone.

"Dad, should I make you some hot chocolate?" I ask him.

"Thanks, love."

Mom and Aunt Hettie take Grandma to the main floor guest bedroom where they shower her, and I go into the kitchen to make everyone a hot chocolate. I want to leave Lesley out but I don't dare because it'll just cause trouble and I want tonight to be good. Although Mom always gets stressed when she invites people over, her parties are great.

I stir the hot chocolates and take a tray into the living room.

"You better have made me one," Lesley threatens.

I can't answer back because right at that moment Mom opens Grandma's door and Aunt Hettie leads Grandma into the living room. They lower her down into the sofa next to Lesley in front of the log fire. Anger flashes through me when I see Lesley frown—she looks disgusted—and she mutters, "Great," under her breath as she stands up.

"You've grown, dear," Grandma says to Lesley.

"*Whatever!*" she says, as she walks away.

Grandma stretches her swollen ankles out in front of the fire. She sounds as if she's slipped into a place where no one can reach her, as she stares at some holly that decorates the fireplace.

"Oh, is it Christmas? I just love Christmas. In Ireland we used to leave Santa a mince pie and a glass of sherry, when I was a girl. And we used to leave Rudolph a sprout and a carrot. He gets hungry, you know, traveling all around the world." Grandma looks away from the fire towards us, and says, "And who wouldn't? I know I'd be hungry if I had to deliver presents to all the kids around the world. Have you got any chocolate, Hettie?" She turns to me and says, "I love chocolate, dear."

"I'll get you some," I say, and go to rummage through a tin of Christmas candy to find some that aren't too chewy. Grandma has false teeth, and Mom reminds me that they won't stay in place if I give Grandma a caramel. I hand her a small bowl full of soft centers and her eyes light up.

Dad sits next to Grandma, rubbing his hands to bring the life back into them. He starts to tease her.

"Are you going to eat all of those chocolates,

Grandma? Share one with me. Y'know your daughter's starving me. We're not allowed any treats when you're not here. I think you should move in."

"When, dear?"

I can't help but smile. Mom shakes her head but Aunt Hettie laughs.

"Oh, I think you should stay," Dad says.

"Stay where, dear?"

"Anywhere that there's chocolate."

"Oh, me too," Grandma says, stuffing another soft centered chocolate into her mouth. "What did you say your name was?"

It hurts me to hear Grandma ask Dad what his name is, but he doesn't seem to mind. He's kind and continues to plays with her.

Mom and Aunt Hettie head off towards the kitchen to begin preparing food for the party, and within half an hour they've transformed the dining room into a fancy buffet.

Mom tells me to go upstairs and change. I shower and wear my new outfit. I fix my hair and swivel in front of the bathroom mirror, put a coat of lipstick on, and go downstairs to meet Mom and Dad's friends.

I feel a little self-conscious so I busy myself by hanging up coats, and then I wander around with trays of fancy party food, offering them to the people who fill our house.

Dad's in the corner talking to his boss, Carol.

She's wearing a backless red dress and she lo
like a model. I can't help but think that she must
cold.

I walk over to them with a tray of goodies an
wait for Dad to introduce me to her.

"Maizy, this is my boss, Carol. Carol, this is my
beautiful daughter, Maizy," he says, sounding awkward. He glances around and says, "Maizy, have you
met Carol's son, Ronan? Oh, there he is." He nods
towards a guy who's about my age, and Dad embarrasses me by calling out, "Ronan, come and meet
Maizy."

Ronan cuts his way through the guests who are
packed like sardines in our dining room, and he grins
at me.

"Hi," I say, flushing, as he thrusts out his hand.
I shake it with my free hand, which has suddenly
gone clammy. I'm terrified I'll drop the tray.

"I haven't seen you before," he says, demanding
an answer.

There's no way that he goes to my school because I would've noticed him. He's gorgeous, and
as I think it I feel crushed knowing that he'd never
look twice at me. I mumble and feel stupid when he
asks me to repeat myself.

Just then Lesley pushes past me and holds out
her hand to Ronan. He looks shocked when he sees
my double.

"I'm Lesley," she says in a voice that tells me

o. Every part of me is on edge and
...shes into my mind and I realize that
...ving in on Ronan as she did on Mark.
...arts spinning badly. My face burns with
...d jealously when I hear Lesley turn on her
..., silky voice, the one she keeps for getting
... she wants. I can't stand it so I walk away to get
...oda. My hands are trembling and I lean against
...ne sink, take a deep gulp from the can, and try
to control the hatred that flows through me. I feel
powerless. She had to have been watching me, for
the moment I looked at Ronan and thought he was
gorgeous, she was there at my side trying to push
her way in.

The evening's over for me and I just want to get
out of here. I drain the can of soda ignoring the
fizzing in my throat and nose, and head towards my
room. But just as I put my foot on the first step,
Ronan taps my arm.

"So, your name's Maizy and you have a twin sister," Ronan says obviously. His face is red.

"Yes," I say, with a bitter edge to my voice. "Oh,
yes, I have a twin sister."

"You're incredibly alike."

I can feel my face slip into an ugly frown. "Maybe
in looks, but that's where it ends."

He cocks his head to one side quizzically, like
he's trying to figure me out.

I'm so bitter inside that I can't hide the hatred

I feel, as the memories of Lesley flirting with Mark in front of me on our birthday flood my mind. Am I to face this every time I like a guy? Is she going to push her way in and take him right before my eyes? I can't bear it. I frown at him, not caring if I'm being rude, I just want to go to my room and cry. I don't want to allow myself to feel attracted to anyone if I end up feeling this bad. It's not worth it.

I put my foot on the next step and he grabs my arm. "Don't go. Stay."

Suddenly Lesley stands right behind him and she tugs on his shirt. "Hey, where are you going? I've made you a cocktail." I look at the two fancy glasses in her hands. She grins at him and tries to hand him one. "Mom says we can only have the punch that has no alcohol in it, but I put some in. Cool, huh?"

I know my face betrays what I'm feeling. Ronan looks at me and then at Lesley as she offers him the glass.

"Thanks, but no thanks," he says coldly, turning away from her. He looks at me, demanding a response as my foot hovers on the third step. "D'you want a non-alcoholic cocktail?" he asks, and suddenly his face is alive. "I make a mean cocktail, y'know. Well, actually, it's more like a fruit salad," he laughs. "It's pretty, though," he adds in a goofy voice that masks a plea.

I look at the two glasses Lesley's holding, each with a solitary cherry in it, and I feel a giggle come over me as I picture a glass of shimmering punch over masses of fruit.

I look at Lesley. She looks like a thunder cloud. She didn't expect this and neither did I.

Ronan totally ignores Lesley and reaches out to take my hand. This time she hasn't ruined it for me. I follow him through the crowd.

He grins at me and says, "Okay, this is it." He picks up two glasses and spoons in loads of fruit from a tray next to a shrimp ring. A giggle seeps out of me as he assumes the pose of a TV chef and talks in a French accent. "Anz next ve add zee pineapple and zee mango, no?"

He hands me a glass that really does look more like a dessert than a cocktail and I laugh. He grins at me and holds out his glass to clink mine and we take a sip. It's very fruity and sweet. Out of the corner of my eye I see Lesley glaring at us, but I don't care.

The rest of the evening goes by in a heady whirlwind, and when Mom hisses in my ear to take a tray and circulate through the crowd, Ronan says he'll take one, too. We wander together, me giggling and him wising off, offering food to people. Lesley is everywhere. She's like a demon, a hallucination, always there, but her whispered voice drenched in hatred is real. She's mad at me, and mad that Ronan hasn't fallen for her "charm." Several times she comes over to us and has a fake high-pitched laugh that she used when she was with Mark on our birthday. She tries her hardest to get Ronan's attention, but he and I have the giggles and no one else matters.

I feel as if I've died and gone to heaven. My whole world is his smile, and his smile is only for me. It's not for Lesley.

Mom is like a butterfly flitting from one group of people to the next, and every time she comes near me she hisses orders in my ear. "Take that tray over there. Go round and fill people's glasses. Don't forget to make sure Grandma's all right."

I do as she asks and Ronan helps me. I lead him over to the sofa where Grandma's sitting in front of the fire.

"My grandma's a bit confused," I warn him. "Mom says she's got dementia. She's gotten loads worse since my grandpa died. It's sad really, but she's lovely," I say, hoping he'll be kind to her.

"My grandpa died of that, too," he says. "It was awful. It was as if we didn't know him in the end and he didn't know us, either. When it first started he used to get so angry if he couldn't remember what he was trying to say, but as he got worse, it was a bit easier on him because he didn't realize that he was forgetting things. I know that sounds weird but that's how it was. It was harder for us, I think," he adds, lost in his own thoughts.

We sit either side of Grandma and she looks surprised but pleased.

"Isn't the fire nice?" she says smiling, her top teeth slipping a bit.

I glance at Ronan to see if he's grossed out but he just smiles at her. Something swells in my heart—he's gorgeous.

"What d'you want for Christmas?" he asks her conversationally.

She looks at him with surprise on her face. "Is it Christmas, dear?"

"Yes, it's Christmas," he says kindly.

She starts to repeat herself about when she was a girl and tears fill her eyes. I pat her hand, not really knowing what to say. "What's wrong, Grandma?" I ask lamely.

She sounds like a child. "I left my Christmas stocking at home," she cries, as if she's stuck in a place far removed from our living room, and our time. "I haven't got anything to leave Santa, either," she wails.

Mom turns away from the person she's talking to and frowns. She heads towards us quickly.

"Shhh, Grandma," I urge. "It'll be okay. I'll get some milk and cookies for Santa. You can leave them by the fireplace."

I can tell Mom is irritated. "What's going on?" she demands. "What have you done to Grandma?"

Ronan glances at Mom and I see a flicker of a frown on his face that tells me he thinks she's being unfair. He stands up for me. "Grandma was reminiscing about Christmases when she was young. We were just going to get her some milk and cookies to leave out for Santa."

"And a carrot for Rudolf," Grandma says excitedly, suddenly lucid.

"Yes, and a carrot for Rudolf," Ronan adds, winking at me.

Grandma cuts him off and starts to whine, looking at Mom. "Where have you put my Christmas stocking, you naughty girl? Just wait 'til your father gets home."

People start to stare and Mom looks awkward. Lesley sidles over to the sofa, smirking, obviously glad that Grandma is making a scene. But as Mom opens her mouth to say something to the people glancing our way, Ronan grins at me and leans towards Grandma to get her attention.

"It's all right. I've got a special Christmas stocking for you to hang up," he says, patting her hand.

"You have?" Grandma's face suddenly shines. Lesley rolls her eyes as others gather around the sofa to see what all the fuss is about.

"Yes, I have," Ronan says, pulling off his shoe and sock. I stifle a giggle as he sniffs his sock dramatically, saying, "Hmm, not *too* bad."

The giggle escapes me—I can't help it. Mom is quiet as everyone mutters about how wonderful it is to see a young man care about the elderly. Then Mom recovers and tries to help.

"C'mon, Mom," she says, "let's hang it by the fire."

She turns to her friends and whispers, "She can't help it, poor thing."

I can't help but think that Mom didn't need to say it. Perhaps she's embarrassed. I'm not; I love my grandma, and I would do anything to make her happy, even play along with the Santa and Rudolph thing.

Mom takes Ronan's smelly sock and pins it above the fireplace. Grandma watches but seems to forget that Ronan has just given her his sock for when she sees his bare foot, she cries out, "When I was a girl we were poor, too. My mother couldn't afford to buy us socks, either."

I start to giggle and Ronan laughs, but Mom rolls her eyes.

"Someone get the boy some socks," Grandma demands. "It's Christmas. No one should be without socks at Christmas. Look at mine. I've got cozy socks." She stretches out her legs and wriggles her toes inside white furry socks with blue balls on them.

Mom wanders back to her friends and Lesley sits next to Ronan. With a flirtatious smile, she coos, "Why don't you come with me to get Grandma some milk and cookies, Ronan?"

Ronan glances at Lesley and me, obviously wanting to do the right thing but that would mean following Lesley.

"It's all right, Lesley," I say pointedly. "We've got it. Why don't you go and enjoy yourself?"

My face and voice are cold and harsh. I want her to go. She's trying to ruin everything for me.

Ronan takes my lead. "Thanks, but we were just about to go and get the milk and cookies," he says, trying to head her off.

"Y'know, Maizy is so good with old folks," she manipulates softly, "that she should stay here to keep Grandma calm." She shakes her head convincingly, enjoying herself. "It would be awful if Grandma was to get upset at Christmas."

I feel sick and Ronan looks defeated. "I won't be long," he falters, as he stands to join her. She gloats at me behind his back as they head towards the kitchen.

I stretch my neck to watch them. Jealousy flares inside me when Lesley slips her arm through his. My heart is racing. She's doing it again, trying to steal the guy I like. I feel hopeless and full of hate and anger, yet right this minute I can't do anything about it, as I can't leave Grandma. I want to scream. Mom will be mad if I leave her and she starts to freak out again. The injustice eats away at me when I think of Lesley, who doesn't care who she hurts so long as she gets what she wants, compared to me, stupid me, who feels screwed up when my grandma is confused trying to recapture the magic of her youth.

I can't think straight—I don't hear a word Grandma says—and my hands are trembling by the time they come back with the cookies and milk. Ronan leads the way with a plate of cookies and he looks irritated. Lesley's almost running behind him carrying a glass of milk, as he strides towards me.

Suddenly the room seems to come back into focus, my hands stop trembling, and my thoughts drop into place. Lesley hasn't won him over. I smile at him and my heart soars as he smiles back and sits next to Grandma.

"Here you are," he says. "Is this enough for Santa?"

Grandma's face lights up and she takes a chocolate chip cookie. "Oh, thank you, dear. My favorite."

Lesley hovers above us still holding the glass of milk. I glance at her and suddenly her face twists with revulsion as she looks at Grandma. I turn around and feel grossed out myself as Grandma takes out her teeth and starts to suck on a cookie. I hate the fact that the first thought in my head is whether Ronan will be grossed out too and will walk away. I shoot him a pleading glance and I'm instantly reassured when he stifles a grin.

"Um," Grandma murmurs and takes another cookie in her free hand, as her teeth sit in her lap.

"Are they good?" I ask, as a glob of chewed-up cookie slides down her chin, nestling in her whiskers.

Lesley turns her head in disgust. This is my chance to show Ronan that I'm different from Lesley. I ignore my own feelings of revulsion and smile at Grandma.

"Is it yummy?" I ask.

"It sure looks like it," Ronan laughs, and we share a smile as his eyes lock with mine.

Lesley slams the glass of milk down on the mantel, not caring that it slops over the side and spreads towards the paper garlands Mom decorated the fireplace with. She stomps off, and I give a careless shrug while hiding my feelings of triumph. She gave up; I can't believe it. The jealousy I felt evaporates and a heady glow spreads through me as Ronan smiles at me again.

Eventually Grandma finishes the two cookies and I ask her if she's ready to leave the rest for Santa. She looks startled. "Santa? Is it Christmas? Is he coming? I've been good."

Her words roll off her tongue reflecting the confusion in her mind. It tells us how lost she is inside her head. I grab her hand, trying to anchor her to this moment. I feel sad and sick as anxiety flashes across her face.

"It's okay, Grandma," I say, trying to reassure her. "It's Christmas and we always leave cookies and milk out for Santa. Do you want to put them on the mantel?"

"What?" She shakes her head as if she's trying

to clear her mind of debris. "Yes, yes, Christmas, Santa, cookies. Have you got some carrots for Rudolph?"

Ronan glances at me and the kindness on his face melts my insides. He dips into his pocket and pulls out a bag of washed baby carrots. I want to laugh because it looks so funny. I mean, who has carrots in their pocket? He sees me grinning and says, "I couldn't find a bowl so I brought the bag."

We help Grandma to her feet after she puts her teeth back in and grins to make sure they're in the right place. Several guests stand around the sofa watching as Grandma places the cookies, milk and carrots by the fireplace. My heart soars as I see that no one has the same disgust that Lesley had on her face—they all smile, and I feel proud of my grandma, even though her head is all jumbled up because she's old and has dementia.

Chapter Three

*L*ater Aunt Hettie asks me if I'll help put Grandma to bed, since she's beginning to nod off on the sofa. Of course I'll help, but I feel a flash of panic wondering if Lesley will make a move on Ronan while I'm gone.

I try to hurry Grandma but she takes her time, and I glance over my shoulder to see Ronan going upstairs to the bathroom. Grandma sits on the edge of the bed as we help her into a nightgown. She looks cute nestled into the pillows and snug beneath her comforter. I place a kiss on her cheek and wish her Merry Christmas. It's weird because suddenly she seems lucid. She grabs my hand and says, "Merry Christmas, Maizy. You're so beautiful." But the moment after she says it, she looks vague again, as if she's trying to figure out where she is. Getting old sucks. I want Grandma to be the same as she was when I was little.

Aunt Hettie ushers me out of the room and immediately I look for Ronan. Lesley's flirting with one of Dad's friends. She's gross. I can't see Ronan, so I head upstairs and find him coming out of the bathroom.

"Is she okay?" he asks.

"She's fine," I say, feeling a bit awkward as we stand outside my room. I don't know what to say, so I shrug and open my door. He follows me, scanning the posters around my room.

"Hey, I like them, too. I went to see them on tour. They were awesome," he says, and I'm green with envy.

He picks up one of my books. "Hmm, so you're a fan of Harry Potter? I've read all the books and seen the movies, too. Don't you just wish you had a wand so that you could make the evening last longer?"

I giggle, thinking how cool that would be. "I might make people disappear, or turn them into frogs," I laugh.

He looks suddenly serious. "Who would you make disappear?"

I wish I hadn't said it because he's put me on the spot and I'll feel stupid if I don't answer.

"My sister," I say bravely. I'm scared that he will see the hate in my heart and won't want to be with me. I talk fast, wanting him to understand. "I can't believe that we're so different, or that we're not close. Twins are supposed to be close, but it's never happened. I don't know how we could've gotten to this, but it's always been the same for as long as I can remember." I look at him and I curse myself when my eyes fill with tears. I sit on my bed and he sits next to me.

"It seems like she's constantly out to get me..." I say, my throat closing with pain, "...like it's a game. It hurts so much and I don't understand it. Mom and Dad don't do anything to stop it. Sometimes I think they're scared of her. I know I am."

Ronan doesn't say anything, but he takes my hand. I shrug, feeling hopeless and afraid that I've said too much. I fall silent, aware that my nose is running.

"Your sister is not at all like you, that's for sure," Ronan says. "It *is* kind of weird that you look so alike but you're so different."

He leaves the truth hanging in the air, and after a few moments we face each other and smile. He makes it all right, and suddenly I feel light and happy again.

After a while the noise downstairs changes; the music is turned down and people are talking—they're leaving. Ronan stands and I follow him out of my room. We stand at the top of the stairs and, as all the people are getting their coats and saying goodbye to Mom and Aunt Hettie, he takes both my hands in his and lowers his face onto mine. He smells divine and I lose myself in a heady wave of passion. This is my best Christmas ever.

When the moment finally passes, he draws away, saying, "I'd better get my coat; my mom's about to leave."

We look over the banister to where Mom and Aunt Hettie are helping everyone into their coats, and Ronan's Mom is standing at the back of the line next to Dad. Everyone is hugging each other and Mom tells them to drive carefully because it's still snowing outside. Ronan holds my hand and says, "I'd better go. I'll call you tomorrow, okay?"

I smile at him but then something catches my eye. Carol squeezes my dad's butt. At first I can't believe what I'm seeing, and when I don't answer Ronan, he follows my gaze.

"Oh my..." he says awkwardly. "I guess my mom's had too much to drink. Don't mind her."

I feel embarrassed. There's something not right about seeing grown ups flirting, especially if they're your parents. Ronan breaks them up by coming down the stairs noisily.

"Hey, Mom," he says loudly, "are you ready? I'm driving."

She takes her hand off Dad's butt. I don't know where to look, especially because Dad looks flustered when he sees me standing next to Ronan.

"Well, yes, um, I'll have that ready for you the day after Christmas," Dad says, but something other than work flashes between them.

I stare at my dad and he looks shaken and un-comfortable. I hate what I'm seeing. He backtracks and digs a hole for himself. Carol doesn't seem at all fazed. She just walks over to Mom and allows Mom to hold up her fur coat so that she can slip it on. "It's mink," Carol says loudly, and my jaw clenches. I hate people who kill animals so that they can wear expensive coats, and I hate them even more when they boast about it.

"Wonderful party," she says to Mom. "You'll all come to my New Year's Eve one, of course?"

Mom says, "That would be wonderful. Thanks."

Carol heads towards the door and Ronan follows, mouthing to me, "I'll call you tomorrow. Merry Christmas."

They're gone in a flurry of snow and suddenly the house is quiet.

"What a wonderful party," Aunt Hettie says to Mom, as she starts to tidy up.

My head's spinning. I know I've only just met him but I'm hopelessly in love with Ronan, and yet feel-ings of anger keep intruding into my euphoria. How could my dad stand there and let another woman feel his butt with Mom and Aunt Hettie in the same room? I don't know what to do with my feelings, so I head towards the kitchen to get a soda. I wish I hadn't bothered. Lesley's leaning against the coun-ter and starts on me as soon as I walk through the door.

"Ronan doesn't want you," she laughs. "He's messing with you. You're too *nice*. What would someone that cool want with someone as boring as you? Get real."

I try to ignore her as I open the fridge, but she's determined to get at me. "I mean, look at the way you dress. Look at your hair."

She doesn't wait for me to answer but walks out of the room laughing, pushing past Dad who is standing in the doorway. I don't know what to think. Deep down I believe every word she's just said. Ronan *could* have any girl he wants. Why would he be interested in me? Perhaps he *was* just amusing himself—something to laugh about with his friends. My sense of euphoria begins to slip away from me like water through a sieve, and as Lesley laughs loudly on the way to her room, I feel deflated and stupid.

Dad breaks into my thoughts. "Maizy." He sounds anxious.

"What?"

"Maizy, Carol is my boss. She was just a little drunk, that's all," he adds quickly.

He sounds guilty, but my thoughts are so muddled about Ronan and the things Lesley's just said that I don't pay Dad any attention.

"Come and sit with us by the fire and help fill the Christmas stockings," he says, a little too eagerly.

Any other time I would have enjoyed helping,

but my heart feels heavy and so I kiss Mom and Aunt Hettie, wish them a Merry Christmas and head up the stairs to my room.

Lesley's just coming out of the bathroom and taunts me again by shaking her head, laughing and saying, "Never in a million years—he's making a fool of you."

Tears prick my eyes and I'm instantly irritated with myself for letting her get to me. I cuss at her and she goes into her room, laughing.

I lie on my bed and cry. I feel submersed in misery. How can I feel so high one minute and so down the next? Why do I doubt myself so much? Lesley is full of herself. She's confident and doesn't seem to care about anything. I'm not like that. I don't understand how we can be so different when we're identical twins. We have the same genes. Looking at her is like looking in the mirror, and yet there *is* a difference, it's something deep inside us. I don't get it. I don't understand why we're different.

Thoughts flood my head; Lesley's taunting of me competes with the exquisite memory of Ronan kissing me. My tears stop and a smile settles on my face when I think of his smell, his lips on mine. Then I giggle to myself when I remember Grandma thinking he was so poor that he couldn't afford socks. Just then my phone rings.

"Hello," I say, half expecting Lesley to continue taunting me by phoning from the next room.

"Maizy?" I hear Ronan's voice and my heart soars.

"Yes?"

"I know it's late, sorry, but we just got home and I wanted to say thanks for a great evening."

As we talk for over an hour and I hear Mom, Dad and Aunt Hettie go to bed—the stockings stuffed and the cookies and milk consumed—everything Lesley said to hurt me dissipates. As we laugh and joke around, trying to be quiet, my doubts subside. It's late when we finally say goodbye and I fall asleep instantly with a smile across my face.

It only seems like minutes later when I hear Mom tapping on my door.

"Wake up, girls. It's Christmas morning. C'mon, Santa's been here." I groan but haul myself out of bed when she opens my door and lowers her voice. "C'mon, Maizy, let's make it nice for Grandma."

Every year Mom and Dad fill our Christmas stockings and we play-act as if Santa has really come down our chimney. I don't mind because it's cute. When we were little, Grandma would join in the pretense and I'd be so excited with my bulging stocking. Now that Grandma is suffering from dementia and seems more like a child than a grandma, I want to make her feel the same magic she tried to make for me when I was little.

I pull on my dressing gown, step into my fluffy slippers and head downstairs. There's no sign of

Lesley. Mom calls her impatiently, and when she doesn't reply, Dad tells Mom to leave her in bed and to start without her. Aunt Hettie leads Grandma to the sofa while Dad stokes the fire, making the embers glow and bite into the fresh logs he places in the grate.

"Look, Mom," Aunt Hettie says, her voice a notch higher than normal, "Santa's been here." She helps Grandma sit down and hands her a bulky Christmas stocking.

"Is it Christmas?" Grandma asks, looking confused, her teeth slipping in her mouth.

"Yes, it's Christmas," Aunt Hettie says, glancing at Mom. They share a moment of concern and regret. I feel such sadness in my heart.

Dad hands a stocking to me. "Merry Christmas, Maizy," he says, his eyes staring into mine with something unsaid in his gaze.

I feel awkward but take the stocking from him and mutter, "Thanks."

We sit around the fire making exaggerated cries of delight, pretending to be six years old, desperate to recapture the magic of Christmas. I glance around and feel sad. Mom and Aunt Hettie sit on either side of Grandma and she's the only one that truly looks enchanted, as if the magic is alive for her. Dad keeps glancing furtively at me, and I look away from him because he's making me feel anxious.

The day goes by surprisingly fast. Lesley doesn't get up until lunchtime and leaves her Christmas stocking unopened—her way of letting us know that Santa is for losers. Grandma has lucid moments that come and go—they come out of nowhere and then she forgets where she is and what day it is. Mom gets stressed in the kitchen as she prepares Christmas dinner and snaps at me to keep Grandma occupied. Finally we sit around the table.

As I'm digging into dessert, the phone rings. Dad rushes to get it and I frown at him. He's never that eager to get the phone. He turns to face the wall as he starts to speak but then turns to face us and says, "It's for you, Maizy. It's Ronan."

My face flushes and I ignore Lesley, who scoffs loud enough for me to hear. My heart's racing by the time I take the phone from Dad. Ronan sounds awkward to begin with but then blurts out, "Can I come over?"

Lesley storms off to her room when Ronan arrives and I'm glad. The rest of the day goes by in a heady dream, where Ronan amuses Grandma, and Mom and Aunt Hettie smile at each other, whispering, "What a nice boy," to which I tell them to be quiet.

"The kids got back from Dad's this morning. It's too crazy for me," Ronan tells Mom. "My sisters fight all the time. It drives me crazy."

"We used to fight when we were kids, didn't

we?" Aunt Hettie says to Mom, "but not since we grew up."

"I don't think my sisters will ever stop fighting," Ronan adds. "They seem to enjoy the drama. And they're even worse with Dad's new wife's kids. That's one of the reasons why I didn't go over there last night, well, and because I wanted to come to your party," he says to Mom. He grins at me and I blush. "You may know my sisters, they go to your school." He tries to describe them but I don't recognize them.

It's late when he leaves and I feel a bit irritated because we're never alone, so he doesn't kiss me. Lesley's words lodge in my mind and I try to force them away. Of course he likes me. He wouldn't have come over if he didn't.

It snows the next day, and the next, so our Christmas break becomes extended, and the trees in our garden look like a scene on a Christmas card. Even though the roads are bad, Ronan comes over to our house every day and he comes with me to feed Sooty the cat.

Mrs. White's back from visiting her daughter and she gives me a present. I tell her she shouldn't have but she says she wanted to. "After all, you give people you love a present at Christmas, don't you?" she asks Ronan. She embarrasses me by telling Ronan that she wouldn't be able to manage without me, and I shake my head when she's not looking. I really don't deserve the things she's saying. Ronan just beams at me.

As the week goes on, it seems as if Ronan lives at our house because he's always here. We hang out in my room at times and listen to music. Mom and Dad don't seem to mind when it's loud. Grandma chatters on about dancing to the music of Glen Miller in the war. Dad goes to work saying he's got deadlines to meet. Sometimes I think we're all living totally separate lives under one roof, but I don't care, because all I want is to be with Ronan. He leaves the night before New Year's Eve and says he'll see me tomorrow. As I lose myself in his kiss, I think he's talking about the party at his house and I forget to tell him that I've got a dentist appointment in the day.

I wake up irritable. I mean, who makes appointments on the day when everyone's thinking about what to wear and how to celebrate the New Year? Mom drags me out of bed early because we have to say goodbye to Aunt Hettie and Grandma who are driving home today. I hug them and I feel a bit tearful. Grandma seems so frail. Mom nags at me to get in the car or we'll be late.

The dentist takes forever and my lip feels divorced from my face when we leave his office. I feel woozy from the shot he gave me and I long for my bed.

I sleep for most of the day until Mom wakes me

up with a strong coffee and tells me to get in the shower because it's only an hour and a half until we're expected at Carol's house. As I get ready, I pray that my numb mouth won't embarrass me by making me drool and slur.

Time races by and a taxi arrives at our house. Mom gets in the front and Lesley and I get in the back.

"Where's Dad?" I ask.

"He's already there," Mom says. "Carol wanted him to help decorate her living room for the party. He went straight from work."

I feel uneasy but put my arm across my stomach in an attempt to still my anxiety. Why did Dad have to help? Ronan could have helped his mom. I force my thoughts away from Dad, as Lesley fidgets beside me. There's something on her face that grabs my attention—it's a smirk. I feel as if she wants me to ask her what's on her mind, but I know my sister. I don't trust her, so I say nothing and try to ignore her.

As the taxi crawls along the frozen roads, my heart begins to race. Tonight, I'm going to meet Ronan's sisters, Millie, Molly and Mandy. He told me how pathetic he felt it was for his parents to name his sisters after a song. He thinks that the kids at school give them a hard time and that's why they're so angry and argumentative all the time.

The taxi pulls up in front of a house that shines

and twinkles with Christmas lights. Mom pays the driver. Lesley's still smirking as she gets out of the car and wriggles around in her tight, short skirt to make herself comfortable. I try to ignore her. I guess she thinks she looks hot and I don't. Whatever!

Ronan opens the door and is very polite to Mom. He takes our coats, and just then Carol comes around the corner. She looks stunning—like a fashion model.

"So glad you could come," she says to Mom, but there's something ugly in her voice that betrays the smile on her face. "What a lovely dress," she croons as she walks into the living room, her eyes already on something else. Mom glances at me. Lesley follows Carol. Dad is standing behind a table that's full of bottles and glasses.

He looks awkward, or maybe I'm imagining it. I don't know. Things don't feel right. This party doesn't feel the same as ours when Grandma and Aunt Hettie were there. Dad asks Mom what she'd like to drink. He sounds like a butler. Carol floats off towards the door as more guests arrive.

Ronan takes my arm and guides me out of the living room into a den. There's a wide screen TV in the corner and a group of kids is sitting in front of it playing a game.

"This is Maizy," he says. "And these are my sisters, Millie," he points as he names them, "Molly and Mandy. Maizy goes to your school."

They don't even bother to turn around as they're glued to the TV screen.

"Hi," I say to the backs of their heads, unable to see whether I've met his sisters at school, or not.

"C'mon, let's go and get a soda," he says.

I follow him into the living room and head towards Dad. Ronan pours some fruit punch into two glasses and hands one to me. I follow him as he walks out of the room. I catch sight of Lesley, who is still smirking. What's her problem?

Ronan leans against a wall, holds my hand and looks into my eyes. My stomach does a double flip.

"Maizy, I'm so sorry if I hurt your feelings earlier," he says. His face is deadly serious and suddenly I'm scared. What's he talking about? "It's just that I don't want to mess things up. Yes, of course I want you, but we should wait, okay?"

My mind seems to disintegrate as I figure out in an instant what he's talking about. I didn't see him earlier; I was at the dentist. Oh, God—Lesley. What has she done? She's hit on him. How far did they go? Now I know why she's been wearing a smirk on her face ever since we got into the taxi. I don't know what else to say other than blurt out my feelings.

"I was at the dentist this morning, and I've been in bed for the rest of the day."

"What?" Ronan cries as he shakes his head. "No. You were with me. We nearly..."

He looks freaked out.

"No, I was at the dentist with Mom all morning and then I went to bed," I say, my eyes brimming with tears.

Lesley walks over to us, triumphant. She steps between us and puts one arm around Ronan's waist, and the other around his neck as she croons seductively into his face. "Baby, you were *so* hot today. You kiss like a dream. Next time, baby, next time, right?"

Hatred flares through me more vividly than ever before and I can't stop myself—I slap her hard across the face. She doesn't even look surprised but just laughs more loudly as she thrusts her face into mine, hatred alive on her face.

"It was *so* easy," she jeers as she steps away from us. "All I had to do was to act nerdy and he bought it."

I feel as if my heart's going to burst; it's racing with fury. Ronan shakes his head and I see contempt on his face. "Stay away from me," he calls after Lesley, her laughter still ringing in our ears as she wanders into the den where the other kids are still playing video games.

He swallows hard. "I didn't do anything with Lesley, I swear," he says. He takes a deep breath. "I guess I don't understand what's going on between you two." He looks at me long and hard and says, "Maizy, I really like you. I haven't done anything wrong."

I look into his eyes and know he's telling me the truth. Then he looks at me and shakes his head as if he doesn't understand. "How can you be identical and yet be so different? She's hateful. I mean, my sisters get on my nerves all the time but I'd never do anything to hurt them."

"I don't know," I say. I look at the anguished look on Ronan's face and feel an overwhelming wave of love wash over me. He thought that *I* was offering him sex earlier today and yet he didn't take it. I've heard in the locker room at school what other boys want from girls, and I feel blown away that he didn't take it when it was offered on a plate. All the anger coursing through my body disappears as I melt beneath his gaze. I lean into him and he puts his free arm around me, trying to avoid spilling his fruit punch.

Music blares out and the guests are dancing. We just melt into each other and his kisses chase my sister's betrayal away. She can't touch us.

Carol asks Ronan if he'll take over for Dad to keep everyone plied with drinks. I go with him to help. Everyone's going crazy as the evening goes on and the New Year approaches. The music's loud and people crowd around the table while Ronan and I try to keep up with their requests. Ronan's little brother, Timmy, gets under our feet. I send him off with a tray full of potato chips to hand out to guests and he seems happy, needed, so he leaves us alone.

I chop more fruit to put into the fruit punch and I fill up the ice bucket. Ronan glances at me and smiles. He's gorgeous. This is going to be the best New Year ever.

Just then I hear someone yelling, and goose bumps spring over me as I recognize Mom's voice.

She barges through the crowd towards me and she looks wild, crazy.

"Get your coat, now. We're going home. Where's Lesley?" Spit flies from her mouth and her eyes are wild.

"What's wrong?" I ask, feeling scared.

"Your father, that's what's wrong," she shouts.

Someone turns the music off and her words echo around the room. She looks at Ronan as if he's an alien, which is weird because I know she likes him.

"Your slut of a mother is *doing it* with *my* husband as we speak," Mom spits at Ronan.

"What?" we ask together. She must be wrong, but as she yells and cusses and says terrible things about Carol, I know she's telling the truth.

"We're going home, right now," Mom instructs me. "Get Lesley. We're leaving, now!"

I don't know what to do. We don't have a car here. We came by taxi. Mom's already turned around and is heading for the door, without bothering to find her coat.

Someone turns the music on and the guests turn back towards the table with all the liquor on it.

"Help yourselves," Ronan says, as he follows me through the packed living room. "Wait, Maizy. I'll take you home."

"Mom, wait," I cry, but she's already through the door and bracing herself against the icy wind, desperate to get away from the house. I follow her outside and slip on the packed snow as I try to catch up with her.

Ronan shouts at me, telling me to stop her. He heads towards his car and, as I forge ahead, the wind biting into my face, I grab hold of Mom's arm. As Ronan revs his car and pulls up beside us, Lesley shouts from the door telling us to wait, and I notice that she's the only one wearing a coat.

I push Mom into the back seat of Ronan's car, and I get in beside her because she's so crazy right this minute that I'm scared she'll jump out and do something stupid. My teeth are chattering, I'm so cold. Lesley sits in the front, and even though I'm out of my mind with worry about my mom, I notice the rigid pose Ronan takes when my sister sits beside him. She's quiet and says nothing.

Mom's crying and saying foul things about Carol, which embarrasses me because she's talking about Ronan's mom. He doesn't say anything, though, but sits alert as he drives on the ice. Snow falls and his windshield wipers struggle to clear the glass.

It's ages until he turns into our drive. Mom's still yelling all kinds of things about Dad, bad things—

things about his body and about the way he makes love to her. I'm embarrassed; parents shouldn't talk that way in front of their kids. She sounds like she hates him and I feel confused. I hate what he's done, but he's my dad.

The moment Ronan stops in our drive, Mom yanks open the door and stumbles out into the snow. I'm glad that Grandma isn't here anymore because she'd be worried, but I wish that Aunt Hettie was still at our house because I need her help. I don't know what to do with Mom. She's gone crazy.

She staggers through the snow as Ronan parks the car, and I try to run after her but she's too fast. She fumbles with the lock and opens the door, screaming all the time, foul things about Dad. I hate it and I'm scared because I've never seen her this way before. Lesley shoots up the stairs to her room and doesn't come out.

Ronan appears in the doorway, his car keys in his hand, and stamps the snow off his shoes on the door-mat. He looks worried. Mom's rummaging around in the kitchen, looking for a glass and a bottle of gin.

I watch her, feeling helpless as she pours herself a large gin and tonic water. My stomach churns as I realize that she never drinks gin because she says that it makes her crazy. She takes several deep swigs from the glass, draining it, and then ignores us as she goes up the stairs. Within minutes she stumbles down the stairs, her arms full of Dad's clothes. She yells the whole time as she barges past us, opens the door and heads toward the snowman Aunt Hettie made yesterday. She dumps Dad's clothes in a pile and then sprinkles something over it. I assume it's lighter fluid because when she drops a match to it, it flares instantly and my dad's things burn until they are cinders. And all the time Mom's screaming like a crazy woman, telling the whole neighborhood what she'd like to do to my dad, and worse, what she'd like to do to Ronan's mom. I'm embarrassed and afraid.

Chapter Four

Tears pour down my face as I try frantically to force Mom to come inside the house and to calm down.

"C'mon," Ronan urges, taking Mom's arm. "You'll freeze out here."

Mom turns on him and hisses into his face, and I can barely make out what she's saying—something about being the "spawn of a whore." She sounds totally crazy. I follow him and grab her other arm, and between us we lead her away from the fire as she yells and sobs.

I only realize how cold I am when we finally shut the door and the warmth in the house envelops me. My teeth chatter and I'm shivering all over, but that's nothing compared to Mom. She's wearing her favorite backless dress and she looks blue with cold. I run into Grandma's room and grab the comforter off the bed—it smells a little of lavender and urine—and as Ronan forces Mom to sit in front of the glowing embers in the fireplace, I throw the quilt around her.

She looks up at me, small, like a deranged clown. Mascara is smudged all over her face. She starts to rock backwards and forwards, howling. Ronan and I share a worried glance. I've never seen an adult fall apart before and it's scary when it's your mom. I try to comfort her, but she looks from Ronan to me and pushes the comforter away and stomps off towards the kitchen as we follow helplessly.

It's like I don't even know her anymore. I feel scared. Lesley's nowhere to be seen. She's in her room and I hate her even more for not caring enough to try to help. Mom reaches for the gin bottle, and as she yells and cusses about Dad and Carol, she fills a glass with liquor.

"No, Mom. Don't. You'll get sick," I plead.

She cusses at me and takes a swig of gin. I'm afraid. I know that people can die from drinking undiluted alcohol.

"Mom, please. Put some tonic in it, or something. Please," I beg, but she just staggers towards me with the glass of gin in her hand, and something foul and ugly settles on her face.

She raises the glass in front of my face, so close that it almost touches my nose, and says, "To your father and that whore."

Ronan flinches but doesn't say anything. I feel

awful, and I try to grab the glass from her hand. The gin slops over the side as we grapple for the glass and it falls to the floor, seemingly in slow motion. Time reverts back to normal as she slaps my cheek hard, rage visible on her face.

"You bitch," she screams at me, turning back towards the gin bottle. She doesn't even bother to get a glass, but gulps deeply, as if she's desperate to finish the bottle before we can stop her.

Tears roll down my stinging face, and Ronan puts his arm around me. "Leave her," he says. "You can't stop her."

I cry like a baby and I follow him back into the living room. I sit on the sofa while he rekindles the fire. Flames lick the firewood he places strategically on the bed of glowing embers, and then he places a log gently on top. He sits next to me with worry etched on his face.

"She's an adult," he says wisely, "and she'll do what she wants to. You can't stop her. She'll pass out soon and then we'll make sure she's all right." He stares at the flames beginning to leap around the log. "My uncle died after drinking too much liquor—he vomited after he passed out and inhaled it. My Grandma found him the next morning lying in a pool of vomit, blue and cold."

"I'm sorry," I say, feeling bad for him, but even more worried. I'm so grateful he's here.

I can hear Mom thrashing about in the kitchen,

staggering and bumping into things. Just then a car pulls into our drive. I'm scared. It has to be Dad. It is. He lets himself into the house, glances at me with shame on his face, and heads towards the kitchen where Mom's still cursing.

At the sight of Dad, her cussing becomes a crazed tirade of hate. Instinctively Ronan and I go over to the kitchen. Dad reminds me of a puppy dog pleading for a treat, constantly whining and begging, but all his efforts are wasted as Mom lashes into him, biting him with the hatred in her voice and the betrayal in her heart. We stand in the kitchen doorway, witnesses, hovering, waiting to step in, but helpless as Mom destroys my dad with the thing she says.

Finally we step aside as Dad leaves the kitchen and does as Mom demands—he leaves. My head spins with emotions. How could he leave when he can see how destroyed Mom is? Yes, I know she's just been hateful towards him, but she's hurt and angry. I feel so let down. Not only can I not believe that he would cheat on Mom, but I can't believe that he'd leave the house knowing that Mom is crazy drunk and that I'm going to have to make sure she's safe. What can *I* do? She has just hit me.

I feel cast aside, like I don't matter. Ronan takes charge.

"Please, come and sit down," he begs Mom. "It'll be okay. Please."

Her crying is worse than her raging, and she seems to shrink before us. I take her arm as she staggers incoherently across the floor towards the sofa in the living room. The Christmas lights twinkle on the tree and around the fireplace, and I have the urge to throw them in the trash. They seem to mock us—Christmas is supposed to be about happy families. I don't want to do Christmas and New Year ever again.

I'm so relieved when Mom flops down onto the sofa; at least she's not fighting us anymore. Ronan sits on one side of her and I sit on the other, and that's how we stay the whole night. She vomits twice while she's unconscious, and Ronan reminds me again that's how his uncle died. I shake Mom each time he mentions it, and she moans before sinking back into oblivion.

Ronan stokes the fire throughout the night and we talk. We talk about everything, things I haven't even shared with my best friend, and as the dawn begins to creep across the curtains, casting shadows on the floor, Mom starts to stir.

I put my arm around her and Ronan gets up to make some coffee.

"Mom," I say anxiously. "Are you okay?"

I hate watching her grapple with consciousness and remembering the awful truth of last night. Her face contorts and she bursts into tears, pushing me and the comforter away angrily.

"That's disgusting," she slurs as she breathes in the lavender and urine that surrounds her. She attempts to stand and I get to my feet, prepared to steady her. She pushes me away again and staggers towards the stairs. I follow her, and Ronan comes to my rescue.

"Hey, I'm making you some coffee," he grabs her hand. "C'mon, come into the kitchen."

She allows herself to be led, and within five minutes Mom's downing cups of coffee and she seems to be listening to Ronan, who's talking fast to keep her attention.

We manage to keep her awake for half an hour before she insists on going to her room. Ronan tells me that she'll be okay now because she's awake enough to be able to respond if she should start to vomit. I feel scared but a bit relieved, and I'm glad that he's here to help me take care of her. We take her upstairs and I plump up her pillows so that she's not lying flat on her bed. She's asleep in seconds. I leave her door open.

As Ronan leaves, he kisses me long and hard and tells me everything's going to be okay, but there's something in his voice that fills me with doubt. My dad and his mom have just been caught having sex; how can that ever turn out okay?

I spend the whole day sitting at Mom's open door, making sure that she's okay. Lesley gets up late and sticks her middle finger into my face as she passes me. I'm so tired that I can barely contain the turmoil inside me. I hate Lesley so much for never missing a chance to hurt me, even when I feel compelled to do the right thing and take care of Mom. I hate the fact that I feel *compelled* to take care of people. Why is that? How can Lesley and I share the same genes and yet be so different? She doesn't care at all and I care too much. The pain inside me is unbearable.

Mom sleeps the whole day, and when she finally wakes up, I scoot away from her door so that she won't get mad at me for *spying* on her, and run down to the kitchen. Mom won't let anyone come inside her bedroom. When she comes downstairs there's a hardness on her face that I haven't seen before.

She peers into the mirror and mutters, "Well, if he can do it, so can I."

She picks up the phone and dials. Her voice resembles Lesley's when she wants something.

"Hi, Leo, it's me. How about you come round for a New Year's drink?" She fiddles with her hair as she listens. "No. I've kicked him out. I've had enough of him. He's useless." She forces a laugh.

Lesley walks past me and hisses into my face. "Sucker." I cuss at her but it doesn't make me feel any better. Every time she picks at me I feel as if she's eroding the edges of the very thing that keeps me together. I don't know how much more I can take. Maybe it's because I've been up all night and I'm worried out of my mind, but I feel as if I'm going to explode into a thousand tiny pieces that will disintegrate and never be able to be put back together.

I turn my back on Lesley, but my stomach churns as I watch Mom flirt on the phone. I don't know who she's talking to.

"See you in a while, then," she says, hanging up. She turns towards me and snaps, "Clean this place up; a friend of mine is coming over."

"Who?" I ask. "Mom, don't do this. What about Dad?"

I've said the wrong thing and she launches into me, ranting on about how weak my dad is and what a slut Carol is. I back away from her because I'm scared she'll hit me again. I can see Lesley laughing at me as she stands behind Mom.

I run to my room and call Ronan. I'm crying really hard, and he tries to calm me down as I tell him that Mom's going to make out with another man, just to spite Dad.

An hour later this guy comes over to our house. Mom has showered and done her hair and makeup, and although she looks nice, there's something predatory on her face that makes her look ugly to me. Leo is loads younger than Mom, wears his hair in a ponytail and hasn't shaved. He's everything my dad isn't.

I'm embarrassed by the way Mom drapes herself over him, and I go to my room and turn my music up loud. Lesley kicks open my door and tells me to turn it down. I cuss at her but she shuts my door, laughing at my ineffective anger. I throw myself on my bed and pull a pillow over my head and scream into it, trying desperately to release the mounting tension inside me. It doesn't do any good, though. All it does is make my throat sore.

I feel like a caged animal, confined to my room. I can't bear to see Mom with another guy, so even though it's snowing outside, I put on my coat and head over to Mrs. White's house.

I feed Sooty and Mrs. White asks me what's wrong. Everything tumbles out of me in an incoherent mess and she frowns at me, trying to make out what I'm saying. "Have one of my daughter's Christmas cookies," is all she says, but I decline because I feel so sick that I couldn't possibly eat. She plays with Sooty with her good arm, and I feel that she didn't understand anything I said, so feeling even more alone, I trudge back home.

I can hear Mom and Leo upstairs. I feel disgusted. How could she, with Lesley and me in the house? I turn the television up really loud and flick channels but can't concentrate on anything. I feel so angry—angry with my dad, Carol, Mom and of course, Lesley. I wish Aunt Hettie were here. She'd know what to do.

I'm just about to pick up the phone to talk it over with her, when I hear Dad's car pull up. Panic flashes through me and I run to the door to head him off. The look of anger on his face tells me that he knows Mom's not alone. Ronan must have told him. He doesn't even bother to stamp the snow from his boots as he comes through the door and glances around the living room.

"Where is she?" he demands.

"No, Dad. Don't!" I cry, grabbing his arm, scared that there's going to be a terrible scene.

He pulls away from me and heads up the stairs.

"Dad," I cry, uselessly, waiting for what's about to happen.

The house seems to erupt with screams of anger and accusations. Leo appears at the top of the stairs in his underwear, trying to defend himself as Dad punches him, and Mom is screaming at Dad, slapping him around the head. She looks crazy, swinging at Dad in just her bra and panties, her hair flying everywhere. Lesley comes out of her room, slips passed them, and comes downstairs. "Party time," she laughs, enjoying the chaos.

Just then a car pulls up and I pray it's Ronan. Lesley opens the door, and to make things worse Carol stands at the bottom of the stairs demanding that Dad leave with her. When Mom sees Carol, she stops slapping Dad, runs down the stairs, and starts laying into Carol, who calls Mom "trailer trash" and says it's no wonder Dad doesn't love her anymore. Mom's mouth is foul and she says words that I didn't even know she knew. She appears so deranged that she doesn't even look like my mom anymore.

I run to the phone and call Aunt Hettie. I'm so relieved to hear her voice, but I'm crying so hard that she can't understand what I'm saying.

"What's going on?" she shouts repeatedly.

As Mom knocks Carol to the floor, I hang up the phone and rush to pull Mom away from her. Dad grabs Mom, too, and Carol scrambles back from her in an undignified tangle of arms and legs, her stocking tops showing. A bizarre stray thought pops into my head—*whoever wears stockings other than pole dancers?* She struggles to her feet, pulling her skirt down, limping, as one of her high heels has broken off.

Leo reappears at the top of the stairs, now dressed, and he slips quietly out of the house as Mom and Carol continue to yell insults at each other. Dad tries to get in between them, but they push him out of the way as if he's insignificant, and they vent themselves on each other.

The phone rings and it's Aunt Hettie frantically asking what's happening. I cry out an explanation and have no idea if she can hear me or not because Mom and Carol's yelling steps up a notch as their hatred for each other flares up and spills over. I can't hear Aunt Hettie, so I hang up again, as there's no point in trying to listen. It rings again immediately but I leave it. Lesley picks it up and laughs into the phone, "Happy New Year," and leaves the receiver on the table so that Aunt Hettie can hear the commotion but do nothing about it.

I feel as if my world is falling apart. I can't take it anymore, so I run upstairs to my room, slam my door, and lean against it panting hard. Why did Ronan tell Dad that Leo was here? I feel as if I'm locked inside a crazy nightmare, and I pray with all my heart that I'll wake up and it'll be Christmas Eve again, with me waiting for Aunt Hettie and Grandma to arrive.

I use my cell phone to call Ronan, and all my frustration pours out. "Why did you have to tell my dad that Mom was having another man over? Don't you know what you've done?" I cry. He's very quiet as everything spills out of me. "Your mom's here and they're fighting. I trusted you. I didn't think you'd go and tell Dad. You've made everything worse."

"I'm sorry you feel that way," is all he says before hanging up on me. I redial immediately but he doesn't pick up, and I feel so desolate that I throw myself on my bed and sob.

I hear Dad and Carol leave and Mom yelling out of the door. She tells him that she's going to divorce him and take everything he has. She cusses at Lesley as she goes to her room, and I hear her rooting through Dad's closet looking for more things to destroy.

I'm so tired but I can't go to sleep until I've spoken to Ronan, so I call him again but one of his sisters tells me he's gone out. I don't believe her. I feel hopeless, and eventually cry myself to sleep.

I awake, my stomach cramping with anxiety, and call Ronan again but the answer machine comes on. I don't leave a message. I'm besieged by doubts. Perhaps what Lesley said was true after all—Ronan wasn't really interested in me.

Aunt Hettie comes over and I'm so relieved to see her, but Mom screams at her when she says that having Leo around isn't going to help and tells her to leave. I watch her leave from my bedroom window, feeling empty and set adrift with my own misery unrelieved.

The day goes by and Mom is more hateful than Lesley is, so I try to stay out of their way. I give up trying to call Ronan because I don't want to humiliate myself anymore. If he doesn't like me, so what? I try to bolster myself up, yet my thoughts don't help; I still feel more miserable than I've ever felt in my life. I hear Mom shouting at Aunt Hettie again, this time on the phone, and I imagine that my aunt is trying to talk Mom out of doing anything rash. It's too late, though, because I hear Mom talking to her lawyer about a divorce.

I wander about as if I'm a zombie. I help Mrs.

White and finally accept one of her Christmas cookies as she chatters on at me; I wash her dishes and tidy up for her. Sooty nestles into my lap and I stroke her absentmindedly, oblivious to what Mrs. White is saying, my mind full of Ronan and his absence.

It's three days before he comes to see me, and I don't know if I'm relieved or angry with him for hanging up on me and ignoring me for days. I know I'm sorry for blaming him and I tell him so. When Mom sees him, she flips out.

"Get out of my house!" she yells. "You're not welcome around here anymore!"

"Mom! It's not Ronan's fault," I defend him.

He shrugs and turns around to leave. I shoot Mom a hateful look and follow him outside.

"I wanted to come over," he says, "but I felt bad. I told your dad you were worried, but I didn't think he would come over, and I can't believe that Mom came over. I thought you blamed me for the fight."

"I'm sorry. I just didn't know what to do. I still don't," I say. "What's going to happen?"

He shakes his head. "I don't know. Mom says it's serious. I don't know how to tell you this, Maizy, but Mom says she's been seeing your dad for months. I swear I didn't know. Mom found out two days ago that she's pregnant."

"What!"

"I know. I can't believe it either. She's pleased.

I'm not," he adds. "I didn't know what to say. That's why I didn't call you. I'm sorry."

My head swims as I take in the things he's saying. A baby will be my brother or sister and Ronan's brother or sister—that's not right. Ronan's my boyfriend, but a baby will make us like brother and sister. What if Dad and Carol get married? We *will* be brother and sister. Tears well up in my eyes as the truth settles over me. I'm crazy about Ronan, but thanks to my dad and his mom we can't be together. A warm tear rolls down my chilled face and Ronan looks as miserable as I feel. He puts his arms around me and I can't help it, I sob.

"Why did this have to happen?" I finally manage to say, my ragged breath coming out in misty spurts. "It's so unfair. We didn't ask for any of this."

He leaves and I go back inside the house. I feel so much hatred inside me that I can't keep it in. "I hate you," I yell at Mom. "You've ruined my life."

She turns on me and shouts, "Surely you don't expect me to have that slut's kid in my house, do you? Grow up, Maizy."

"Shut up," I scream at her. "You drove Dad away. You were always nagging at him and putting him down. And you're just as much a slut as Carol is."

"Don't you dare say that," Mom shouts, marching towards me with her hand aiming for my face.

I dart out of the way and run up the stairs to my room.

"Get down here!" she yells, but just then the phone rings and she answers it. "Oh, hi Leo. No, I'm sorry about the other night. It's okay, though. Yeah, I've filed for divorce. C'mon over."

• • • •

By Easter my life has totally fallen apart. Mom is divorcing Dad and he and Carol are planning to get married as soon as they can. Mom, Dad and Carol forbid Ronan and I to see each other anymore as boyfriend and girlfriend. My heart's broken and I hate my parents. I hate Lesley more as she taunts me about losing Ronan. I feel so angry and full of hate as Ronan's sisters tell me that my dad is their dad now.

Dad picks up Lesley and me on Sundays and takes us over to Carol's house. I can't stand being around Carol and the girls, knowing that they all live with *my* dad and I don't. The girls hang all over him and call him "Dad," which makes me so mad. Ronan is always out, which hurts, and I ask Dad to take me home early. He always looks uncomfortable yet when Carol insists that we stay for dinner, Dad gives in to her. What I want doesn't matter. I can't stand watching the way Carol bosses Dad around— she treats him just the same way as Mom used to. I get so mad at Dad for not standing up for himself. Lesley seems to relish at my discomfort and actively befriends Millie, Molly and Mandy, hanging out with them in a way she never has with me. When Dad and Carol aren't around, I hear Lesley saying foul things about me to the girls, and they side with her and gang up against me.

Every time Dad drives us home, Lesley constantly begs him for money and he gives it to her to keep her quiet. He offers it to me, too, but I always get out of the car feeling angry, for I feel as if he is trying to buy me. Lesley calls me a loser as she pockets the money before Mom sees it. She bleeds him dry but he won't, or can't, say no. I bet Carol doesn't know that he gives Lesley so much money, and if Mom knew she'd go back to court for more child support.

Time and time again I pray that Mom and Dad will sort it out, but I know it'll never happen because Carol's pregnant and Dad's going to marry her, so my prayers remain unanswered.

Leo moves in and Mom nags him. She wants a baby too, but he tells her that he's had a vasectomy. She gets so mad that she breaks up with him for a week, but then asks him to come back. Mom doesn't want another baby—that's stupid—she just wants to top anything that Dad has. I don't know how Leo puts up with her, because she's constantly ranting on about Dad. If it were me, I'd be jealous, but Leo doesn't say much. Mom's vicious about Carol, saying how fat she's getting, and she takes delight in turning up at the same restaurants as Dad and Carol to flirt with Leo in front of them. How she knows where they're going, I don't know. It's like she's obsessed with Dad. Perhaps if she'd been so into him when they were together, he wouldn't have become involved with Carol.

The worst thing is that Millie tells lies about me to Dad. At school she taunts me and I try to walk away. But then when she goes home she says that I've been mean to her, and Carol makes Dad phone Mom to tell me to stop. Mom and Dad start fighting and then Lesley gets involved and backs up Millie, saying that she heard me being mean, too. Lesley laughs when Mom's not looking, and I feel as if I'm going to burst with anger at the injustice of it all.

I begin to spend more and more time at Mrs. White's house and find comfort in the warmth of Sooty's body in my lap. Mrs. White is a little deaf and I don't know if she can hear me when all my troubles pour out of me, but she smiles at me and gives me a frail hug with her good arm each time I leave.

When I'm at home I spend all my time in my bedroom, and at school I become very watchful to make sure I won't run into Millie in the halls. I feel nervous and anxious. My head hurts constantly and my stomach lurches so much that I need the bathroom all the time. One day I'm hurrying to my last lesson when she and her friends catch up with me.

"I'm telling *my* dad that you called me a bitch and took my lunch money," Millie says, laughing,

"He believes everything I say. You're in *so* much trouble." I hurry along the hall, but she speeds up and grabs my sleeve. "He doesn't care about you anymore. He's my dad now, and my mom's having his baby. My mom says that your mom's a bitch, and she's not surprised that he wants to be with my mom rather than yours."

My head starts spinning and something inside me snaps. I turn on her and start cussing. She slaps me and I slap her back, and then she pushes me. I land on my ass, and her friends laugh at me as I scramble to my feet and run down the hall, trying to get away from their jibes.

I make it to my class and sit there, my heart hammering and my face stinging, not hearing anything the teacher's saying. The lesson is almost over when the school secretary opens the door and tells me I have to go to the principal's office. Everyone looks at me as I get up to leave, and I feel really sick.

I sit in his office, cringing as he shouts at me. Millie sits a few feet away with her face all bloodied and her eye so swollen that it's almost shut. I hear him say that I'm suspended, but he won't listen when I tell him I didn't do that to Millie's face. She swears I did and he believes her.

As we leave the room she mutters under her breath, "Oh, you're in big trouble now."

The bell rings and the halls are suddenly full of

kids making their way to the school gates. I follow them blindly, trying not to cry in front of anyone.

Just as I get to the gates I bump headlong into Ronan. My heart does a double flip and I don't know whether to laugh or cry. But the look on his face is all wrong and I know he's not pleased to see me.

"Maizy, what's going on?" he snaps.

Millie is right behind me and calls out, "Thank God you're here, Ro, Maizy went nuts. Look what she's done to my face."

Ronan looks at Millie's swollen face, and then he looks at me with contempt. "I can't believe you attacked my sister. Y'know, Maizy, you need to grow up. Things happen—that's life. My mom and your dad are together; you have to accept it. Stop taking out your feelings on my sister. She's going to be your sister whether you like it or not."

My mouth drops. I can't believe what he's saying. Surely he knows me better than that. I want to cry. I really thought he knew me. The realization that he doesn't swamps me in a tidal wave of hopelessness and despair. I try to protest but it does no good.

"Y'know, we could all get along, but not if you're going to be like this. You stay away from my sister," he says. "You're sick, Maizy, you need help. You need to get over it."

He tugs on Millie's sleeve and she follows him, but not before glancing around at me with a smirk on her face that beats every one of Lesley's when she gets me into trouble.

I turn the other way, even though it's not the shortest route home, desperate to put distance between us. My head is spinning so badly that I can't be sure what's just happened. All I know is my heart is broken beyond repair and I'm drowning in a sea of injustice, hatred, anger and betrayal.

I walk as fast as I can, praying that I'll bump into something and it'll annihilate me. I don't want to live anymore. It's all too hard. I can't cope. There's a noise in my head that drowns out the sound of my sobbing; I think I'm going crazy. My life's not fair and I just want out.

As I turn onto our road I see an ambulance outside Mrs. White's house. I run down the road, through her front door, to find two paramedics tucking her arms into a black bag, about to pull a zipper over her grey, lifeless face.

The men tell me to go away, and as I back out, my head spinning wildly with shock, Sooty mews at my feet, so I pick her up and run over to my house.

Mom's on the phone and she sounds angry. She tries to lay into me while she's holding a conversation with, I assume, my principal. I stand there holding Sooty, unable to move. She cusses at me and then says into the phone, "Perhaps you can talk some sense into her." She thrusts the phone into my hand.

It's not my principal. I hear Aunt Hettie's voice and suddenly the corroded edges of myself disintegrate and I am no more. Everything becomes a blur except for a distant, small, desperate voice that cries, "Aunt Hettie, help me."

Chapter Five

Mom grabs the phone, pushing me away, and I start to scream. Sooty leaps from my arms and runs away. Mom yells at me to go to my room, but I don't remember climbing the stairs. Everything looks different, and as I catch sight of myself in the mirror, I don't look like me. I look away and throw myself on my bed, pull my pillow over my head, and press my face into the mattress. I want to die. I want the pain to end, but when I can't breathe and my chest hurts, I let go of the pillow and gasp for air. I turn over and stare at the ceiling as tears pour down my face. I can hear Lesley downstairs telling Mom that I hit Millie. She sounds predatory, enjoying the drama, saying that I pick on Millie all the time.

The room spins and I see images of Mrs. White, dead in a black bag, Millie's swollen eye, the contempt on Ronan's face and Lesley's hatred of me, and I'm consumed by grief and anger. Time ceases to have any meaning and my throat's on fire with the roaring that comes from deep within me as my pain has nowhere else to go but out.

Mom and Lesley burst through my door, bolstered by each other. Mom demands to know what's gotten into me and says that she's ashamed of me for getting suspended. Lesley eggs her on and chips in, saying that I embarrass her at school and she's ashamed to be my sister.

Their voices fuse into one long denigrating tirade, where I feel stripped of all that I am, like a wounded animal beneath hungry vultures. As they stand in my doorway, I sit up and push myself into the corner of my room, my knees tucked under my chin, trying to protect myself from their onslaught of hatred. They don't stop, so I clamp my hands over my ears in an attempt to block them out, but all that does is infuriate them. Mom strides across the room and tries to grab my hands away from my ears and, as I grit my teeth and clench my muscles, determined to cover my ears, she roars into my face.

"You little bitch. You *will* listen to me."

Lesley joins her, her face contorted with malicious laughter, and she helps Mom pry my hands off my ears. They're too strong for me, and when my ears are free, their voices sharpen, leaving me nowhere to hide from their animosity.

I can't explain the sudden surge of strength that blasts through me. My legs are kicking and my arms are flailing everywhere, clearing a path between them. I shoot off my bed and make for the door before they can stop me. I tear down the stairs, open the front door, and collide with Aunt Hettie, who's poised with her key to our house in her hand.

I blaze past her and she turns, calling me. "Maizy, stop. What's going on? Stop!"

My heart hammers inside my chest and, although I'm desperate to get away from my house, my family and my pain, something registers deep within me—help is here. I stop, halfway down the drive on a journey to nowhere, and turn around to face her, panting hard. There's movement in the doorway as Mom and Lesley appear, about to chase after me, but they stop when they see Aunt Hettie.

"Maizy," my aunt says softly, stepping towards me, holding out her hand. "Take my hand. Let me help you."

It's as if we are all moving in slow motion. My head is full of noise—recriminations and accusations—and, as I think briefly of Ronan and Mrs. White, tears pour down my face and I begin to howl. Aunt Hettie moves towards me and stretches out her arms in a hug that will save me if I can only reach out. I look at Mom and Lesley standing in the doorway, anger on Mom's face and ridicule on Lesley's, and deep down I know that my aunt's arms are my salvation, but I can't move.

"Maizy, please," Aunt Hettie implores, "let me help you. Ignore them." She nods her head in a slight gesture towards Mom and Lesley, and a subtle, knowing glance links us together and I feel a flicker of hope. She continues to hold out her arms, taking slow, tentative steps towards me, her face alive with concern, willing me to respond.

I don't know whether she reaches me or I reach out to her, but suddenly I'm in her arms, sobbing my heart out as she strokes my hair and tells me that it's going to be all right. Mom and Lesley's protests are white noise in the distance as Aunt Hettie leads me to her car and tells them, forcefully, to go inside.

I don't really remember anything other than Aunt Hettie talking on her phone as she drives. I hear bits of what she's saying. "Hi, Tina, how are you? Yes, I'm fine; well actually I'm not. I knew things were bad for my niece, but I didn't think they were as bad as this. She needs to come to Beach Haven for awhile. Do you have a bed?"

My heart's racing; I don't know what's going on.

"Oh, don't worry, her mom will agree, trust me. You have a bed? Cool. We'll be there in about an hour, okay?" she says.

I stare out of the window, watching trees speed past, and as today's events sharpen in my mind, tears roll down my face.

Aunt Hettie glances at me as much as she watches the road, and she hands me a wad of tissues. When I blow my nose she asks, "Are you okay, honey?"

I nod, trying to be brave, but as fresh tears slide down my face, I shake my head and have to blow my nose all over again.

"Baby, I know things are bad for you at home. I'm sorry I haven't been around since Christmas. My life's so busy. I'm sorry. I'm here now, though. I'm taking you to a wonderful place where people will help you. It's called Beach Haven and you're going to meet my friend, Miss Tina. Don't be afraid. Everyone there will help you, and," she pats my knee, "your parents will have to sort out their mess. None of this has anything to do with you. Do you believe me?"

I shake my head. Of course I don't believe her. I'm in trouble at school because I reacted to Millie's taunting. I hit her, I know, but I truly believe that I didn't blacken her eye. I didn't punch her but I did slap her. I wish I hadn't, but something inside me snapped. I'm ashamed of myself.

"I've been suspended from school," I cry, "for slapping Dad's new partner's daughter." I can't say the word, step-sister. "I didn't beat her up though, I swear. I didn't blacken her eye, but no one will believe me." Tears pour down my face as the injustice of it and the look of contempt on Ronan's face swamps me all over again.

"Honey, *I* believe you," my aunt continues. "You've been caught up in the mess that can happen when there's a divorce and remarriage. Everyone's hustling, trying to figure out what position they have in the new blended family. It can be a real mess for a while—it happens all the time. The only people who can truly sort it out are your mom and dad."

I cry as she talks to me, and my throat is so closed that I can't ask her about it. She chatters on, saying things that don't require an answer and I'm grateful.

Eventually she slows down and turns onto a large drive. Her face is beaming. "Oh, honey, you're going to love it here." She digs me in the ribs, and whispers, "No more Lesley, right?" Then she shakes herself as if in reproach and says, "Oh, I know I shouldn't say that, but I can't believe how different you both are."

Her words comfort me, and although I feel a bit scared as she tells me to get out of the car, a wave of relief washes over me as the thought sinks in—Lesley can't get at me here, nor Millie.

I follow Aunt Hettie towards an old building that has a sign over the entrance, "Beach Haven, a place to rest and grow." She opens the door and we step into a reception area that looks more like someone's living room, except that there are two wide, spiral staircases, one leading from the right and one from the left. They lead upstairs to a balcony and all along the walls are pictures that have obviously been painted by kids.

My attention turns towards a lady who has just come around the corner, past a smiling woman who's sitting in a reception window, waving at me.

Aunt Hettie and the lady walking towards us hug, and I stand there feeling awkward.

"I'm Miss Tina," she says, thrusting out her hand to me. "It's good to have you here, Maizy. Don't look so worried; we'll help you." She pats my arm and says, "It'll be all right, you'll see."

Miss Tina tells us to follow her up one of the spiral staircases, and she takes me along a corridor and into a room.

"This will be your room, Maizy," she says as she opens the door, and sunlight floods the room through an open window. I can smell salt. Aunt Hettie goes to the window and I follow her.

Aunt Hettie gasps and says, "Now I see why this place is called Beach Haven. It's beautiful."

The window looks over a wide, sandy cove where sun sparkles on the water like glittering jewels. A sailboat glides along the horizon and seagulls screech loudly as they swoop towards the water. Others perch on the swings in the playground beneath the window, and still others peck around the grass look-ing for tidbits. I can see kids goofing around on the beach, just beyond a grassy ridge that separates the playground from the beach.

"Those are the other kids here," Miss Tina explains. "You'll work hard in group to sort out your problems, but you'll get a lot of free time as well. Remember, Beach Haven is a place to rest and grow."

She smiles at me and I give her a bleak one in return. I hear a bell ring and watch the kids shake the sand from their clothes and head towards the building.

"It's time for dinner," Miss Tina says. "C'mon, let's go and meet everyone."

We go downstairs and Aunt Hettie gives me a kiss, says that she'll call me, and then leaves. I feel scared but follow Miss Tina along a corridor, and she opens a door with a sign above it saying, "Dining Room." It seems like there are kids everywhere and my stomach does a double flip.

"Listen up, everyone," Miss Tina calls. "This is Maizy. Velvet, you help her, please."

A girl with long black hair comes over to me and smiles. "C'mon," she says, "I'll show you what to do."

Miss Tina leaves the room and Velvet takes me to a long table that has lots of different trays of food on it. A lady in chef's clothes stands behind the table and she smiles at me.

"Have what you want," she says.

I don't feel very hungry as I'm too full of everything that's happened to me today, but I put a bread stick and some salad on a plate, and then follow Velvet towards a round table where other kids are already sitting.

Everyone seems to talk at once and tell me their names and why they're at Beach Haven. I feel a bit overwhelmed as I pick at my salad, trying to take in what they're saying.

"Hi, my name's Lexi," a girl with red curly hair says. "I'm here because my family fell apart after my dad had an affair with my aunt. I couldn't cope with it anymore so my mom brought me here."

"Hey, I'm Rocky," a guy says. "I don't know what happened in my family. Everything was okay until Mom started running around. Dad left." He shrugs and says, "I guess I can't blame him really, but I wish he'd stuck around to protect me and my little sister from the creeps Mom brings home." He stuffs a chunk of bread into his mouth and chews viciously.

"I used to be an A student until my dad ran off with my teacher," a girl says, sadly. "Oh, I'm Harriet, by the way. My parents had the nerve to get on my case because my grades have dropped." She shakes her head in disbelief. "Don't they realize how awful it's been for me at school after everyone found out? It was so embarrassing and the kids picked on me. Who could concentrate with all that going on?"

"You think that's embarrassing," another girl scoffs, "try living down the humiliation of your mom having an affair with the pastor of our church." She looks at me as if I'm an afterthought and says, "I'm Marion," and then goes back to what she's saying. "I had to leave the choir because the gossip got so bad. They said terrible things about Mom—said she'd rot in hell. I haven't been back to church since. What can the pastor teach me about sin if he's screwing my mom?"

She sounds so angry and I look away.

A guy breaks the tension. "Hi, Maizy, I'm Scott. My parents aren't married, but man, the drama is every bit as bad as everything you are saying. Baby-mommas and baby-daddies, drama, drama, drama. I tell you, when I'm old enough to have kids, I'm gonna do it right and not put my kids through all this crap just because I didn't choose the right person to be with in the first place."

"Hi, I'm Marcus. My dad left," a guy says bluntly, glancing at me, but then he stuffs his mouth with fries and looks away.

"So did mine," the guy sitting next to Marcus says, grinning. "Sorry to laugh, man," he digs Marcus in the ribs and makes him choke on his fries, "but my dad left with another man."

"That's not funny, Alfie," Velvet says with reproach in her voice.

Alfie straightens his face and says, "No, I know it isn't, but it's easier to laugh than cry."

"I don't know what Miss Tina would say about

that," Velvet says knowingly, and he falls silent. She turns to me and asks, "Are your parents still together, Maizy?"

I shake my head, feeling awkward as everyone around the table looks at me. "No, my dad cheated on my mom." I have the sudden urge to cry, so I pick up my glass of water and drink, praying that I can gain control of myself in front of all these kids I don't know.

Velvet comes to my rescue and says, "Both my parents had an affair, then remarried and decided that there was no room in their new families for me, so I'm in foster care."

Lexi gets up noisily and heads back to the big table to get some dessert. When she returns, several of the others look at her plate greedily and leave too.

Velvet pats my arm and says very quietly, "It's cool here, Maizy. Things will be okay. It feels strange at first but you'll soon get used to it, and then you won't ever want to leave."

I am grateful to her for helping me. Everything feels very strange and I have an overwhelming urge to break down and cry.

After the others return with desserts, eat them, and take their plates to the kitchen, Velvet says, "We always have a group in the evening."

"A what?" I ask feeling apprehensive.

"A group. You know, where *a group* of people

sit there and talk about things," she answers patiently.

"What things?"

"Well, usually we end up talking about how we feel about our parents' divorces." She sees the terrified look on my face and grins, saying, "Hey, it's not that bad. It makes you feel a lot better knowing you're not the only one who feels a certain way. C'mon, let's go. You can sit next to me if it'll make you feel better."

I follow her up a corridor to a room that has the sign "Group Room" written above it. There are armchairs placed in a semi-circle around the room. Miss Tina is sitting in another armchair in front of a table and a flipchart.

When everyone is seated and gets quiet, Miss Tina says, "Tonight we welcome Maizy to our group." My face burns bright red. "Has everyone introduced themselves?" she asks.

The other kids, who sat at different tables in the dining room, blurt out their names but I'm so nervous that I don't hear any of them.

Miss Tina turns to me and says, "Maizy, tell us why you're here."

I feel mortified. I don't know what to say. My stomach churns and I wish I hadn't eaten anything earlier.

"My aunt brought me here," is all I can think of to say.

A kid scoffs and Miss Tina glances at him sharply before speaking again to me. "But what's been happening to you that has led your aunt to bring you here?" she coaxes.

I remember how open the kids were around the dinner table when they talked about their parents' divorces, so I open my mouth and a squeaky little voice comes out that doesn't sound a bit like me.

"My dad had an affair with his boss and got her pregnant. Mom went crazy, burned all his clothes, and is divorcing him."

Miss Tina prompts me further by asking what happened, and with all eyes looking at me, leaving me nowhere to hide, everything that has happened since Christmas tumbles out of me. Afterwards I stare at my shoes, wishing I could evaporate into nothingness.

Miss Tina breaks the silence and I dare to look up at her.

"It hurts my heart to hear how kids suffer when their parents divorce. Divorce itself needn't be the villain, it's *how* they divorce that matters.

"I thought divorce was a sin," a kid blurts out. "That's what my pastor says."

I glance at Marion, remembering what she'd said about her mom and their pastor. She looks angry and her fists are clenched.

"It's one of the Ten Commandments," another kid says.

"No it isn't," Scott blurts out. "It says that you shouldn't commit adultery, but where does it say you shouldn't get divorced?"

"That's an interesting point, Scott," Miss Tina says, smiling at him.

"I mean, my parents have never been married—they don't believe in it." He pauses and says, "I can see why the Ten Commandments say that *adultery* is a sin, though. The way I see it, adultery means having sex with someone else when you're already in a relationship, married or not. That's gotta be wrong, surely, because that's when people get hurt."

Miss Tina smiles broadly at him. "Times change, not always for the good," she says, "and people's attitude towards marriage and divorce change depending upon their spiritual beliefs, their extended family's perception of marriage and divorce, and also society's response to it."

I see some kids frowning.

"When my grandmother was a young woman, divorce was virtually unheard of, and if you found yourself in an abusive marriage, there was no way out of it. People stayed together even if they hated each other because society and their families would have shunned them, as if they were outcasts, if they divorced. Who d'you think would suffer in a marriage like that?" she asks.

"The kids," Rocky says.

"Everyone," Lexi says sadly.

"Yes, everyone," Miss Tina agrees. "Mom and Dad would be fighting all the time and they'd pick on the kids to vent their frustrations. How awful. Do any of you know how that feels?"

All the kids put up their hand, even Scott whose parents aren't married. I guess he knows what it feels like to get caught in the crossfire between parents fighting.

Miss Tina looks around the room and says, "It's awful, isn't it? The best thing we can hope for when two people fall out of love is that they'll know themselves well enough to accept responsibility for their part in the breakdown, and try to fix it. Love is a fickle friend. Being *in love* is different than loving. To love someone means to want the very best for them, and to help them achieve their needs. Being *in love* is about being so engrossed with someone that you can't think straight—it's like going slightly crazy." She grins at us. "Man, it's awesome."

Some of the kids giggle.

She continues, "But over time that heady feeling settles down and the love between two people grows into something more stable—something deeper and lasting. That doesn't mean that you can't still be *in love*, of course you can, but the love changes. It changes as people grow up. When a couple hits a problem, if they know themselves well enough, they can work things out."

She stands, goes over to the flipchart and writes,

"Know yourself," in big letters, and beneath it, "Accept responsibility and work things out," and then she sits down again.

"If you don't truly know yourself, it's easy to blame the other person in your relationship when things go wrong. 'Know yourself' means just that, knowing your weaknesses, and owning your behavior when you screw up. If you are comfortable admitting that you messed up and acknowledge that you are human—and all humans mess up at times—then there's no need for recriminations or accusations. If you can turn around to your partner and say, 'Honey, I'm sorry, I was wrong,' your partner won't feel like he has to defend himself, or herself, from your anger."

As she speaks I try to figure out what she's saying. If my dad had said sorry for sleeping with Carol, my mom would have not accused him of adultery. My head starts spinning. What is this? It's crap. Miss Tina may be my Aunt Hettie's friend but she's talking trash. My face flushes, no, it burns, and I can't believe what comes out of my mouth.

"That's total crap," I blurt out. Every kid looks my way and I wish that I was a shadow of myself, something that could slink away from this room, from their faces that demand an explanation for my outburst. Miss Tina's eyes hold me in her gaze. I want to look away, but I can't.

"Tell me, what is total crap?" she asks, using the

words I wish I hadn't uttered. They are raw, honest, and laid out in front of me and every kid in the room. I don't know how to answer, but I try.

"How can you say that if my dad said he was sorry for having sex with another woman, Mom wouldn't have to accuse him? That's crazy," I cry. "She *should* accuse him, he was in the wrong." But as I say it, doubt floods through me. Everything feels wrong. I know my dad was in the wrong, but I love my dad so much and I know deep down that he's a good man. It can't be this black and white. I feel awful because I don't understand. Mom had every right to be angry. I know I would be if Ronan slept with another girl. Tears fill my eyes as Ronan pops into my head and I remember the scathing look on his face when he believed I'd blackened Millie's eye. He was wrong. Dad was wrong. Was Mom wrong, too? Why is everything so complicated?

I shake my head as images of Christmas Eve spring into my head. Mom had nagged Dad all day. She nagged him everyday. He did everything he could to make her happy but it had never been enough, no matter what he did. I remember him being blue with cold that day, chopping logs for the fire and helping Grandma out of Aunt Hettie's car. Mom didn't help. She stood in the doorway, nagging Dad about Grandma's hip replacement. Mom had put him down every time she could, and she didn't stop Lesley from bad-mouthing him either. It's always been the same for as long as I can remember—Mom always picked on Dad and treated him like dirt, and he let her. Why? I don't understand.

Miss Tina speaks softly. "Maizy, when two people love each other and want what's best for each other, it would seem impossible for either to cheat with someone else." My face feels contorted. "Can you think of a reason why your dad cheated on your mom?"

Something bursts inside me and everything about the way Mom treated Dad cascades from me in a wave of despair. There's a noise that fills my ears, and it's only when I feel Velvet's hand on my back that I realize the noise is coming from me. There is no beginning to myself and no end. I feel fractured and scattered in the wind, every part of me destroyed, doused in images of Mrs. White's dead body, Sooty who couldn't stand to be in my arms, Ronan who thought so badly of me that he believed I could hurt his sister, Mom and Lesley who always think the worst of me, and Dad who lets me down every day because he can't stand up for me when his wife and my mother bully him. His betrayal has nothing to do with adultery, but everything to do with his abandonment of me.

Chapter Six

Miss Tina doesn't say anything until I stop crying. No one does, and gradually my sobs subside. I feel crushed with embarrassment. Finally she speaks.

"Maizy, while you're here at Beach Haven, we'll help you understand why your parents behaved the way they did, and we'll help you to see that their decisions had nothing to do with you. So many children of divorced parents feel that they are in some way to blame, but this is absolutely not true."

Velvet hands me another tissue and I smile at her bleakly.

Miss Tina continues talking. "Relationships are like a bed. Whether or not it will be comfortable and support you will depend upon your behavior. " She grins and says, "You can poop in your bed (be mean and hateful) if you want to, if that's how you treat people, but it's still your bed, your relationship, and you have to lie in it. Gross, huh? Personally, I'd rather have my bed, my relationships, be comfortable, supportive and cozy, but to have that I need to know myself, and I mean *really* know myself."

A couple of the guys are still giggling at the thought of pooping in the bed and Velvet frowns at them.

"Knowing yourself is like embarking on a journey, one that takes a lifetime," Miss Tina says. "It's an adventure." She sees some of us frowning and she smiles. "Trust me, it is," she adds.

"When two people get married and make vows to each other, they usually mean them at the time, at that stage of their personal journey, but if they haven't come very far and don't know themselves very well, when they run into problems, perhaps they don't have the self-insight to be able to accept responsibility for their part in the breakup."

I think quickly as Miss Tina talks. I don't think Mom has any—what did she call it—self-insight, because although Mom blames Dad for everything, she nagged him to death and always put him down. I don't think Dad has any self-insight either, because he never stands up for himself and has hooked up with a woman exactly like my mom. How dumb. He might just as well have stayed with Mom and be nagged, as split our family up and be nagged by another woman, and then I could still be able to go out with Ronan. Tears prick my eyes as I think of him.

"That doesn't excuse their behavior," Miss Tina says, bringing my thoughts back into the room, "as everyone's responsible for their *own* behavior, but it may help you understand why some people just don't seem able to work things out."

So my mom and dad don't have self-insight. Great. How does that help me?

She seems to read my mind and says, "I have a favorite saying, 'There's no blame, only understanding.' When you try to understand things, why two people behave the way they do, it takes away some of the blame and anger that you may feel when things don't work out the way you want them to."

I blurt out. "But I *don't* understand, and I *do* blame my parents, and Ronan's mom, too," I add, feeling my jaw clench with anger.

Miss Tina looks at me kindly and says, "I know, my love, it hurts, doesn't it? We'll help you to see it differently, and we'll help your parents to work it out, too, if they'll let us."

"You're too late," I say bitterly. "Carol's having Dad's baby."

"I didn't mean that we can turn back time," Miss Tina says. "What's done is done. You say that there's a new baby on the way, right?" I nod miserably. "What we hope for when couples divorce and remarry is to help everyone involved to have their own special and valued place in the new blended family."

"Fat chance in my family," Lexi scoffs.

"And the way to achieve this harmony," Miss Tina says pointedly, ignoring her with a smile, "is to *know yourself*, listen to others and respect their point of view and their feelings, while expressing your own respectfully."

Miss Tina stands up and writes on the flipchart, "Why do people behave the way they do?" and sits down again. "This is what we'll explore tomorrow. Okay, let's stop now. Why don't you guys show Maizy around?"

Everyone gets up and leaves the room, all chattering at the same time, and I follow them. Miss Tina pats me on the shoulder as I pass her and she says that she's glad I'm here.

The kids go through a side door that leads to the playground I saw from my bedroom window. A couple of them hang out on the swings, but I tag along with Velvet and Lexi who head towards the beach. There's a warm breeze blowing my hair about as I run over the grassy verge and slip on the loose sand beneath my feet. The girls yell as they run towards the shore and I do the same. It's beautiful here. Although my heart is heavy with all that's happened today, something settles over me as I slip my shoes off and wade in the warm sea. I want to wash everything away, all the pain and hurt. I'm glad that I don't have to go home tonight and, although I feel a bit shy around kids I don't know, I feel safer with them than I've felt all year. We wander along the shoreline, the waves gently lapping at our ankles, and then we flop down on the warm sand beside Scott, Marcus and Rocky.

The kids giggle and goof around, and as they joke, some of my stress ebbs away like the receding tide. Mom, Lesley and Millie seem far away, and I allow myself to sit quietly beneath the screeching seagulls that swoop above us. Images of Mrs. White sneak into my mind and take me by surprise. It dawns on me that she is dead and I'll never see her again. She was the one person who had been my safe haven for years, my lifeline when Lesley's venom became too poisonous and Mom got onto me, but she's not going to be there anymore. Tears prick my eyes as the kids around me hoot and holler, and I quickly brush the tears away, praying that no one notices.

"What's wrong?" Marcus asks me. Everyone turns to look at me.

"Nothing," I lie.

"C'mon," Lexi coaxes. "What's the matter?"

"My friend died today," I cry, and I tell them what Mrs. White means to me. "I can't believe that she's gone."

When I finally stop crying, I feel a bit better.

So much has happened in one day that when it's

bed time, I'm relieved. I nestle into my crisp, clean sheets and pillows and a smile slips onto my face. I feel safe, and sleep steals over me.

All too soon I'm awakened by the sounds of the girls getting ready for breakfast. I rub the sleep out of my eyes and head for my shower. It feels awesome to stand beneath the steaming jets of water without Lesley yelling at me to get out. I towel dry my hair and comb it through. I think it looks awful, so I bend over and shake some life into it but shrug at my reflection as it settles in a scruffy mess.

I feel a bit awkward because I don't know what I'm supposed to do, but I follow the girls down our spiral staircase and walk through the reception area to the dining room. It smells great. I line up with the others to eat sausage and pancakes, and the room is full of chatter. When we finish, I follow Velvet to the Group Room.

"We always have group in the mornings," she explains.

Not again, I think, but I don't say anything as we file through the door and sit down. Miss Tina is waiting for us.

When we get quiet she points to the flipchart and repeats the words she wrote last night, "Why do people behave the way they do? Y'know, libraries around the world are full of books and journals that try to explain human nature and human behavior. Academics and lay people argue whether a person's behavior is due to his genetic makeup or his environment—it's called the great nature versus nurture debate. It's easy to miss the point amidst all those books and scholars arguing, when it seemed so simple to me." She looks around the room and says, "Sorry guys, but I'm going to repeat myself for Maizy's sake." She looks at me and adds, "We worked on this last week but you need to know it so that you can understand why people behave the way they do."

I nod and sit up straight, wondering what she's going to say.

She talks to me and I try to pay attention. My face is burning.

"From the moment of birth to the moment of death, human beings seek Strokes. A Stroke is anything someone does or says that lets you know you exist." I frown and she continues. "Strokes can make you feel good or bad. Dr. Claude Steiner, a very clever man, called positive Strokes 'Warm Fuzzies,' because they make you feel valued and loved and cozy inside. He called negative Strokes 'Cold Pricklies,' because they hurt and make you feel cold and miserable. The point of telling you this is because human beings need Strokes, for they are as important as the air we breathe, and people will do almost anything to get them."

She suddenly looks really serious. "If Cold Pricklies make you feel bad, why would anyone seek them? Why wouldn't everyone seek Warm Fuzzies that make you feel good? The answer lies in what happens in your family. If parents don't know how to give Warm Fuzzies—hugs and kisses, praise and compliments—their kids will seek the only Strokes available to them: Cold Pricklies. It seems that people find it easier to be mean, snappy or defensive than to be open, sweet and kind. Remember, everyone seeks Strokes all the time because it lets them know that they exist. Little kids learn very quickly that any Stroke is better than no Stroke, better than being ignored, so if they can't get Warm Fuzzies they'll act out to get a reaction from their parents, who are likely to be irritated or angry. The more often they get a reaction, the more they'll repeat that behavior. It's called learned behavior—simple, isn't it? So, children's behavior is related to whether they receive Warm Fuzzies or Cold Pricklies and, in turn, how they interact with others shapes their personality."

Velvet turns to me when Miss Tina pauses, and says, "Yeah, and the worst thing is that even babies learn how to get their parents' attention and change their behavior so that they get their needs met." She glances around the room looking for backup from the other kids. "Miss Tina said so," she adds, and then she grins, "It says so in all the libraries around the world."

Miss Tina laughs, "It's called research. Academics study these things so that we can benefit from what they learn. In this case we learn that children grow up to be happier and healthier if they're given Warm Fuzzies rather than Cold Pricklies. Families are happier, too."

My head starts spinning as everything Miss Tina says seeps into my brain and I try to apply it to my own family. My family is miserable. Does that mean that we only give each other Cold Pricklies? And as I think it, it becomes obvious to me. Of course our family is miserable, that's *all* we give each other—Cold Pricklies. Lesley's mouth is full of them. Everything she does with her body, her callous shrugs, her middle finger stuck in my face, are Cold Pricklies. Mom screams at me and sends me to my room because Lesley gets me into trouble—she's full of Cold Pricklies, too. Then sadness washes over me as this new language fills me with knowledge. My dad gives me Warm Fuzzies sometimes. Mrs. White always gives me Warm Fuzzies; she's always nice to me and makes me feel good and cozy inside. As images pop into my head of her sitting by the fire with Sooty on her lap, tears spring into my eyes, and when Miss Tina hones into me and asks me what's the matter, I fall apart all over again.

Velvet pats my back when Miss Tina comes over to me and hugs me. She croons in my ear, saying it'll be okay. I guess she's giving me some Warm Fuzzies.

She searches out my eyes and forces me to look into her face, which I don't want to do. I just want to disappear. "It's tough, isn't it? But there's hope. We can teach you and your families to stop swapping Cold Pricklies and to start giving Warm Fuzzies. It just takes some practice, that's all."

I shake my head and blurt out, "No, they'll never change. My sister is the meanest person I know, and Mom is so stressed that she's mean, too." I know that my dad could learn, though. He's kind inside, I know it, even though he went off with Carol who is also full of Cold Pricklies. She's sarcastic and mean. Millie's the same; actually, Millie's worse. Miss Tina's right, it *is* simple. Warm, cold, love, hate.

Miss Tina goes back to her chair and we all look towards her. She looks at us for a moment and then smiles. "The bottom line is that if you are the kind of person that only gives out Cold Pricklies, no one will like you, and they'll see you as an unsafe person to be around. People will eventually leave you. But if you can learn to give Warm Fuzzies, you'll be happy and everyone will like you. They'll feel safe around you and will want to be with you. That's the bottom line, okay? Simple, right?"

Most of the kids nod and I do too, because as everything she's said opens my eyes, I understand. If Lesley keeps on being mean, no one will want to be with her. Dad left because Mom was mean. When I think about it all, something dawns on me. I have a choice. I've been eaten up with hatred towards Lesley and Millie, and I know I've given out Cold Pricklies to them. But if I don't change I'll be no better than them, and I know deep down that I'm more like my dad inside. I try. I really do. I try to help people. I try to be good and kind.

Miss Tina asks me if I understand and I say, "I think so."

"Remember, a Warm Fuzzie is anything that someone does or says to you that makes you feel good, and a Cold Pricklie is anything that someone does or says to you that makes you feel bad," Miss Tina emphasizes. "If children can't get Warm Fuzzies they'll seek Cold Pricklies, as any Stroke is better than no Stroke. That's it in a nut shell."

I'm thinking as she recaps what she's just told me. I get it, but I also feel troubled. Miss Tina sees me frowning and asks what's on my mind.

"Well," I begin, thinking out loud, and trying to ignore all the kids who are looking at me. My face is burning but I speak out anyway. "What happens if you're nice to people who are determined to be hateful to you?"

"Who are you talking about?" Miss Tina asks.

I tell her about Lesley and how, even though we're identical twins, we hate each other. When she frowns, I quickly tell her that I've always wished we were close like the other twins at the twin conference, but Lesley seems to take delight in hurting me. I'm so mad at myself when I start crying all over again, as I blurt out what Lesley did with Mark and then Ronan.

"Even if I were nice to her all the time, she would still be hateful to me," I cry. "What should I do?" I ask helplessly.

Miss Tina smiles at me kindly, and says, "Ah, that's where your 'personal journey' comes into being. You can only change yourself and hope that in doing so you'll invite other people to respond towards you differently. You can't change anyone else. It's really important that you realize this, because trying to change someone else is futile."

I shrug, still feeling hopeless because I *know* that Lesley won't change. I'm not saying that I'm not going to try to give her Warm Fuzzies, but how can I take it if she's continually mean to me when I'm trying to be nice to her. I try to express what I'm feeling and it all comes out in a jumbled mess.

Miss Tina says, "Don't worry, sweetheart, we're going to help you practice staying okay when someone chooses to be mean to you. No matter what someone says to you, you don't have to retaliate; you can learn to ignore what they say."

The door opens and a lady comes in and the kids call out, "Hi, Miss Cassie."

Velvet whispers in my ear that Miss Cassie is our Life Skills teacher and she's awesome.

"Are you finished with them?" she asks Miss Tina.

"Yes, just about. We were talking about learning to ignore Cold Pricklies," Miss Tina says.

"Oh, you mean dodging them," Miss Cassie says, grinning.

"Exactly."

"C'mon, guys, let's go," Miss Cassie says.

We all follow her out of the Group Room, down the corridor, and into a classroom that has several kitchenettes around the room and deep sinks in a corner.

Lexi tells me that Miss Cassie teaches all kinds of things, including cooking, sewing and art.

Miss Cassie tells us to sit around the big table in the middle of the room and she heads towards a shelf and retrieves a large box. Alfie jumps up to help her. I wonder what's inside the box.

Miss Cassie holds up her hand to get us to quiet down, which we do, and then she says, "Today we're going to make hearts."

"What?" several of the kids say.

Miss Cassie grins as though she has a secret. "We're going to make heart-shaped shoulder bags." She tips out the big box and lots of fuzzy material of different colors and patterns spreads across the table. "You will make a fuzzy bag that will represent your heart, so choose a color and pattern that you think best reflects how you see yourself."

The kids start sorting through the material and I join in. It reminds me of the garage sale we once had where three little old ladies had fought over Mom's old curtains. Alfie and Velvet each tug on the end of a bright red piece of fuzzy material that has black lightning forks over it.

"I had it first," Velvet says. "That's just how I see myself." She grins at Alfie and he messes with her by tugging at it before letting go.

"Well, on second thought, I think this purple one with music notes is more me," he quips, retrieving an awesome piece of fabric.

Lexi holds up a bright yellow piece with fruit on it. "Um, this is me, I think. Bright, sunny and fruity." The boys snicker, and Miss Cassie shoots a playful frown at her.

I sort through the fuzzy material and find a piece that catches my eye. It's lilac, gentle and peaceful. I'm not sure that it represents how I see myself, in fact maybe I should fight Velvet for the red and black piece, but it's how I *want* to be if only I have the chance. I feel the fur slide over my fingers and it feels warm and cozy. I put it to my face and it feels like my old teddy bear. Comfort settles over me and I know I've made the right choice. Lilac it is.

Miss Cassie calls above our chatter and tells us to sit down when we've made our choice. She hands out pieces of heart-shaped paper and tells us to fold our fabric in two and pin the paper to it, leaving a long strip of material to the side. I glance at the others to make sure I'm doing it right and carefully stick the pins through the paper and fabric. She wanders around the table to make sure we know what to do and wags her finger at Scott who cusses when a pin pricks his finger.

"Man, sewing is for girls," he moans.

"Sexist," Harriet protests. "Just because you're clumsy."

"Ha, ha," he gripes, sucking his finger.

"Right, now you're ready to cut out your fuzzy bags," Miss Cassie says, ignoring their banter. "Cut carefully around the shape and then cut the edge of the fabric into a long strap."

Marion has her tongue sticking out as she concentrates and snips around the edge of her paper heart pattern. Rocky takes his scissors and makes bold cuts to begin with but then mutters under his breath when he gets to the hard bits. I take my scissors and cut, praying that I won't make a mess of it. They hurt my fingers as they bite down into the fur, but I persevere and I'm pleased with myself when I see a perfect heart shape in front of me. I watch the others and get the giggles when the guys act indignant just because they've never done anything like this before.

Miss Cassie asks the boys to help her put the sewing machines on the smaller tables that are placed around the room. I've never used a sewing machine before and I feel anxious that I'll mess up, but I needn't have worried because Miss Cassie tells us to gather around and watch as she threads up her machine. She says it's easy and tells us to practice. I manage it on the third try. I feel pride flow through me as I wait for her to help some of the others who have tied themselves in knots.

She shows us what to do and an hour later we all have shoulder bags shaped like a heart. I've never made anything before and I feel pleased with myself. It's not perfect, but it's fine. Velvet walks up and down the classroom as if she's a model showing off her fuzzy bag. Then Lexi and Marion follow her and the boys start hooting. I laugh. It dawns on me that I haven't had so much fun in ages. These kids are great.

"C'mon, Maizy," Velvet cries, "strut your stuff." Everyone looks my way. I shrug and join in, swinging my hips dramatically and letting my beautiful lilac fuzzy bag bounce as I sway across the classroom. The kids hoot and holler for me and I feel great.

When everyone, including the boys, who need a bit of persuading, have shown off their fuzzy bags, Miss Cassie tells us to sit around the big table again.

"Good job," she says smiling. "Awesome," but then she gets serious. "These fuzzy bags represent your heart and I want to ask you a really important question. 'What's inside your fuzzy bag?' Do you know? Do you know yourself well enough to know what's inside your heart? Is your heart full of Warm Fuzzies or Cold Pricklies?"

Everyone's quiet and tension rolls around the room as we face Miss Cassie's challenge. I try to remember how Miss Tina described them—Warm Fuzzies made you feel good and Cold Pricklies made you feel bad. Right now I feel good, so does that mean that I've got Warm Fuzzies in my heart? I know that when I was at home and at school, I had Cold Pricklies in my heart. I hated my mom, and Lesley and Millie.

No one answers and Miss Cassie fills the silence. "You don't have to answer; it's just a question for you to think about." She suddenly brightens and says, "I hope you had fun; it's time for lunch. Leave your fuzzy bags in the Group Room because Miss Tina has something planned for you this afternoon, okay?"

We stream out of the classroom and head towards the Group Room. I put my beautiful lilac fuzzy bag on my armchair and I feel pleased with myself. It looks great. The color catches the light and shimmers, transforming the lilac into silver and back again.

We have pizza for lunch and everyone gives a Warm Fuzzie to the cook. She beams and says, "I know, my loves, it's your favorite. I hope you like it." I take my plate and sit down, thinking, trying to work things out in my head. She just gave us a Warm Fuzzie, too. She's being kind; I like her.

We hang out on the playground after lunch. A couple of the kids run down to the beach but I'm too full to run anywhere. I sit on a swing and sway gently—the color lilac fills my mind. I don't really hear what the kids are saying; they're bantering—I can tell by the back and forth—but it's just noise to me as my mind is full of Miss Cassie's question.

A bell rings and all the kids abruptly stop chattering and make their way towards the door. I follow them, jolted from my thoughts, through the door, up the corridor into the Group Room. I retrieve my beautiful lilac fuzzy bag, that's supposed to represent my heart, and sit with it on my lap. Miss Tina is already seated in her armchair and Miss Cassie pulls up a chair next to her. No one has to tell us to get quiet, we just do.

Miss Tina smiles at us and I realize that she's just given every one of us a Warm Fuzzie. I can't help my face—I send one back to her—I smile.

"You all did an awesome job this morning. Look at your fuzzy bags; they're beautiful."

Miss Cassie beams as she looks around the room. "I'm so proud of you all," she says.

Miss Tina says, "Me too. And now we're going to answer Miss Cassie's question, 'What's inside your fuzzy bag?' Everyone, sling your bags over your shoulders."

We do as she asks, and then she and Miss Cassie share a secretive glance and head towards several boxes on a table pushed against the wall behind them. They fumble and then turn to face us, their arms full of little beanbags.

Miss Tina explains. "The ice-cold blue beanbags are Cold Pricklies, and the yellow ones are Warm Fuzzies. We are going to interact with each other, and when you get a Warm Fuzzie or a Cold Pricklie, I want you to put it in your fuzzy bags."

Before anyone can comment she picks up a yellow beanbag and hurls it at me, saying, "Maizy, I think you're awesome to have survived your mom and dad's divorce." I manage to catch it and put it in my lilac fuzzy bag. Next she throws one to Velvet, and says, "I think you are wonderful for being so strong when you were put into foster care." She and Miss Cassie lob yellow beanbags to us all, saying nice things about each of us, and before long I've got several in my fuzzy bag. Yes, Warm Fuzzies make you feel good, but then Miss Tina frowns and her face contorts. She shocks me when she turns to Miss Cassie.

"Miss Cassie, you're a bitch," she spits, venom alive in her voice as she throws an ice-blue beanbag at her. Nobody moves. I feel my stomach churn with anxiety. Suddenly I feel as if I'm back at home where everyone is slamming each other with hatred. Tension hangs in the room.

Miss Cassie catches the blue beanbag and puts it in her fuzzy bag. She takes a blue beanbag out of the box, saying, "It takes one to know one," and she hurls the blue beanbag at Miss Tina, who catches it and puts it in her own fuzzy bag.

Miss Tina smiles at us and the tension in the room dissipates. "Miss Cassie and I have just exchanged Cold Pricklies. So I have Warm Fuzzies and Cold Pricklies in my fuzzy bag, in my heart."

They go around the room giving each of us five blue beanbags. I don't want them because I guess what she's about to make us do.

"Okay, how did it make you feel to receive the yellow beanbags, the Warm Fuzzies?" she asks. Everyone says that they felt good. "So now experience what it feels like to give and receive Cold Pricklies. Velvet, choose five kids to be mean to. Throw them a Cold Pricklie."

I don't want to do this. My stomach's churning.

"Do I have to?" Velvet asks.

"Yes!"

She looks miserable, but turns to Lexi and mumbles, "Your hair's a mess," and she throws a blue beanbag, which Lexi catches and puts in her fuzzy bag. Velvet turns to Miss Tina and looks close to tears. "I don't like it," she cries.

"Go on," Miss Tina insists.

"You're a fat cow," she says to me, and I catch the blue beanbag and put it in my fuzzy bag, along with the yellow ones that are already there. My stomach continues to churn and I feel really bad. Velvet looks pained as she throws her last three Cold Pricklies out to three other kids. Then we each have to do the same, and when it's my turn I find that I just can't do it. It hurts too much. Miss Tina tells me I must, and so I put Lesley's face on five of the kids and remember some of the hateful things I've said to her in the past. My face is burning and I know it's contorted with anxiety and pain.

When each of us has thrown our five Cold Pricklies away, Miss Tina speaks out. "How do you feel?"

We all speak at once. "Awful."

"Take a look inside your fuzzy bags, your hearts. What do you see?" she asks.

"Warm Fuzzies and Cold Pricklies," several kids call out.

"Yes, so that means that you have a choice to make when you interact with others. You can give out Warm Fuzzies, which will make others feel good and people will want to be around you, or you can give out Cold Pricklies, which will make people feel bad and they won't want to be around you. It's your choice."

She turns to Miss Cassie again and I see a grin flash between them. Miss Tina lobs a blue beanbag at Miss Cassie and says something really mean, but rather than catch it, Miss Cassie dodges to one side and it lands on the floor behind her.

Miss Cassie turns to us and says, "Just because someone throws a Cold Pricklie at me doesn't mean I have to accept it. I can ignore it and then it won't be in my fuzzy bag, in my heart." She reaches into her fuzzy bag and takes out a yellow beanbag. "I can try to make things better between us by offering Miss Tina a Warm Fuzzie..." she throws the yellow beanbag to Miss Tina who catches it and puts it in her fuzzy bag, "... and hope that she'll see how nice it makes her feel. Then perhaps she'll want to give me one back." Miss Tina retrieves a yellow beanbag from her fuzzy bag and throws a Warm Fuzzie back to Miss Cassie, which she catches and puts into her own fuzzy bag.

They make us laugh as they rush towards each other and hug.

Miss Tina grins at all of us and then tells us to practice swapping Warm Fuzzies, and suddenly there are yellow beanbags flying across the room from every angle and we crack up laughing, as a warm, fuzzy feeling spreads throughout the room.

Chapter Seven

That night I snuggle under my covers and think about everything Miss Tina and Miss Cassie have taught me. Miss Tina's question, her challenge to us all, "What's inside your fuzzy bag, your heart?" lodges in my head and won't go away. I toss and turn thinking about it. I think about "knowing myself" and what that means to me. It's all very raw and there doesn't seem to be anywhere to hide from the truth. I can't escape the fact that I've had Cold Pricklies in my heart and I've given them out freely to Lesley, sometimes to my mom, and to Millie and Carol. But I know that I have Warm Fuzzies in my heart too, as it's easy to be kind to Aunt Hettie, Grandma and Mrs. White. It was easy to give Ronan Warm Fuzzies too, until he accused me of blackening Millie's eye. He gave me a Cold Pricklie by mistrusting me and thinking that I could do such a thing. It hurts, but then I think about what's inside his fuzzy bag. He obviously had some Cold Pricklies in there waiting to get out. Questions form in my mind. *Where did he get his Cold Pricklies from? Who gave them to him?* I know where mine come from—the constant battering from Lesley, day in and day out. I guess Ronan got his Cold Pricklies from his family just as I did. I turn over, punch my pillow into a comfortable shape, and will sleep to smother my thoughts.

I awaken starving and shower quickly, looking forward to breakfast. I stand in line with my plate in my hand. Scott pushes in front of me and I feel affronted. He's just given me a Cold Pricklie. Marcus steps aside and asks me to go before him. I smile at him, feeling suddenly shy. He's just given me a Warm Fuzzie.

"Thanks," I say, giving him a Warm Fuzzie, too. He smiles at me—another Warm Fuzzie—and I smile back. I imagine our fuzzy bags beginning to fill to the brim with wonderful Warm Fuzzies. I make a mental note to examine my fuzzy bag, my heart, to make sure that no Cold Pricklies are lurking there, waiting for me to throw them at people who get on my nerves or who hurt me. I don't want to spread shivers and hatred around, even if people are mean to me. I know it'll be hard, but I'm going to try to do it. I want my heart to be filled with Warm Fuzzies because they make me feel so good.

Marcus follows me to a table and sits next to me. He jabs a fork into his sausage and stuffs it into his mouth. He chews frantically, and I get the feeling that he wants to talk to me but also wants to satisfy his hunger. I guess the sausage wins. I fill my mouth with scrambled eggs and look away from him, praying that I haven't dropped any on my chin.

Eventually when the sausage becomes mere crumbs of stray meat around his teeth, he speaks. "Did you sleep well?" he asks awkwardly, sounding like my dad.

I shake my head. "No, my head was full of everything Miss Tina and Miss Cassie told us yesterday."

I look at him as he stabs another piece of sausage with his fork, but he holds it in front of his mouth, about to say something. "Me too. It was, um, right on the mark, wasn't it? I mean, how can you kid yourself that it's everybody else's fault when you are forced to see that you've got Cold Pricklies in your fuzzy bag? My dad left and I'm so mad at him that I just know I've got Cold Pricklies in my heart over what he did. But then, I have Cold Pricklies in my heart for what my mom did, too." He stuffs the sausage into his mouth and chews furiously.

He makes my head spin with his honesty. I feel that he expects me to answer. "Me too. I know I've got Cold Pricklies in my heart for my sister. She hates me, she always has. I don't understand why, but that's how it is."

Marcus continues. "But I've still got lots of Warm Fuzzies in my heart for them both. They're my mom and dad after all. I love them." He shrugs and tips syrup over his pancakes.

"I feel a bit like that," I say. "I mean, I hate what my dad did too, and I know I have Cold Pricklies in my heart because of it, but I still love him. Things have gotten so bad between me and my mom, though, that I haven't got any Warm Fuzzies for her." Now it's my turn to shrug.

Lexi has been sitting next to us throughout and suddenly she turns to me and says, "Yes, but if you try to give out Warm Fuzzies to your mom and sister, perhaps things will get better between you all."

I feel a flash of irritation. I've been trying all my life.

Lexi continues, "Miss Tina says that we can't change other people, remember, but we can only change ourselves and hope that we invite others to respond differently."

Marcus glances at her and says sarcastically, "Oh, how wonderful it is to be so smart."

My mind races. What's sarcasm? It can't be a Warm Fuzzie, surely, even though Lexi grins at him. Is it a Cold Pricklie? I don't know. I look at her, wondering what she's going to do and Miss Tina's words echo in my head. We each have a choice as to how to react to others. She sticks out her tongue at Marcus but he doesn't retaliate. We get quiet, eating our breakfast, and thoughts race around my head. Lexi just gave Marcus a Cold Pricklie by sticking out her tongue, but he dodged it and didn't retaliate by saying or doing anything back. I wonder, if we were still lobbing beanbags about in the Group Room, whether Lexi would have more blue ones in her fuzzy bag than Marcus has in his.

Lexi walks off to dump her tray in the kitchen and Marcus looks at me. I don't have the heart to tell him that he has tomato ketchup on his chin. The sight of him trying to be so serious but wearing a red, shiny emblem tickles me. I giggle.

"What?" he asks, and when I finally tell him, playfulness arrives on his face and digs its heels in. We exchange a series of Warm Fuzzies, and my heart is soaring by the time we dump our trays and head off towards the Group Room.

I sit next to Velvet and when Marcus smiles at me from across the room, she whispers, "He likes you."

Heat flares through me, and I whisper back, "Don't be silly."

She grins at me and says, "I'm right."

Miss Tina silences us and prevents me from answering her.

"How are you all?" she asks. "Have you been thinking about what you learned last night?"

Most of the kids say they have. I do, too. She looks around the room and for some reason hones in on me. "Maizy, tell us what you understand about Warm Fuzzies and Cold Pricklies."

I begin to stutter as I open my mouth to answer, thinking out loud.

"Um, I, er, I think I understand. I hated the Cold Pricklies we shared last night, but I liked the Warm Fuzzies." She doesn't say anything and her silence tells me that she wants me to say more. "I'm a bit confused about one thing, though."

"What?" Miss Tina asks.

"Well, I think I can recognize what Warm Fuzzies or Cold Pricklies are, but what is sarcasm?" I glance between Marcus and Lexi and ask them if I can use what they said at breakfast to illustrate why I'm confused. They both look puzzled but nod. Perhaps they've forgotten what they said.

"We were talking about our feelings after our parents split up and how we know we've got Cold Pricklies in our hearts over it. I told Marcus that things have gotten so bad between me and my mom that I haven't got any Warm Fuzzies for her. Then Lexi said that if I tried to give out Warm Fuzzies to my mom and sister perhaps things would get better between us." I glance at Lexi and hope she's not mad at me for bringing up what she said. "I felt irritated by what she said," I confess. "It felt like a Cold Pricklie but it didn't really sound like one. Then, I felt more irritated when she quoted you by saying that we can't change other people, we can only change ourselves and hope that we invite others to respond differently."

I look at Lexi and shrug, saying, "Sorry."

She shrugs, too.

"Then Marcus said something sarcastic, which made Lexi smile," I go on, "but I would have thought it would make her mad. That's why I'm confused."

"What did Marcus say?" Miss Tina asks.

Marcus looks apprehensive and I wish I hadn't started this.

"He said, 'Oh, how wonderful it is to be so smart,' which would have irritated me but Lexi just smiled. So, is sarcasm a Warm Fuzzie or a Cold Pricklie?" I ask.

"That's a very interesting question," Miss Tina says. "What do you all think, Lexi and Marcus? What was going on inside you at the time?"

Lexi speaks out, "I was trying to be helpful. I thought that maybe, because it was new to Maizy, she might need some help in understanding it all. I know I did when we first learned about Warm Fuzzies and Cold Pricklies." She turns to me and says, "I didn't mean anything bad by it, honest."

I feel terrible and tell her I'm sorry.

Marcus turns to Lexi and says, "Actually, I think you were being sarcastic and you sounded like a smart-ass, so I was being mean when I was sarcastic back, yet you laughed."

Miss Tina smiles and says, "Well, isn't this interesting. So the things you said were either a Warm Fuzzie or a Cold Pricklie depending upon how they were received, not by your intent. What would make one person interpret the opposite meaning?" She looks around the room and no one answers. They look as confused as I am.

Lexi ventures to put her hand up. "In my family everyone uses sarcasm as a joke. I just thought Marcus was goofing around."

Marcus then looks as if he's had a brainwave and says, "Oh, I think I get it. In my family everyone's very critical and quick to tell me what I'm doing wrong. So when you started telling Maizy what she should be doing, I wanted to tell you to shut up, so I was sarcastic rather than saying what was on my mind."

Miss Tina beams at him and says, "Good job, Marcus. What great insight you have. You too, Lexi."

Marcus's words ring a bell with me and I speak out. "I felt really defensive, Lexi, when you told me what I should be doing, and maybe it's for the same reason as Marcus. My mom and my sister constantly pick on me, and I interpreted your advice as you getting onto me."

"Can you see then that each person's perspective, depending on whether they see other people as being safe or not, influences whether they see something as a Warm Fuzzie or a Cold Pricklie?" Miss Tina says. "I think that most Warm Fuzzies and Cold Pricklies are obvious; they either make you feel good or they make you feel bad. But when you use sarcasm, that's when it all gets confusing. Personally, I don't think that anything said sarcastically can ever be a Warm Fuzzie. I think that families who have learned to see sarcasm as funny do so because they don't know how to be close to each other in an honest way, and so they resort to swapping quips about each other. Then if one or the other gets upset about it, they can absolve themselves of any responsibility for their behavior by saying, 'Can't you take a joke?' which puts the blame for the bad feeling onto the victim rather than the person who was saying something mean."

Several kids start nodding, and when I think of all the hateful things Lesley's said to me over the years, I know just what Miss Tina means. When I've complained to Mom and Dad about it, Lesley smirks, saying, "She can't take a joke," and Mom has always nagged at me to lighten up. Lesley would laugh and I'd feel bad.

"Ultimately, sarcasm is a Cold Pricklie disguised as something else," Miss Tina explains. "You may laugh to begin with, or to please other people you're with, but deep down you'll feel bad or unsafe. If you use sarcasm with other people, in time they'll see you as an unsafe person to be with and they may leave you. That's the bottom line. What we hope to do here at Beach Haven is to teach you how to express your feelings honestly without having to resort to using sarcasm."

Miss Tina looks at Marcus. "Marcus, you said that you felt irritated with Lexi yet you didn't feel able to express your true feelings, but they seeped out anyway through sarcasm. You did a good job expressing your real feelings in this group. Well done. I know it's not easy, but everyone here will now trust you just that little bit more because they know that you can be honest in a respectful way."

Marcus beams with pride and I smile at him. I trust him. Velvet glances at me and digs me in the ribs. "Told you," she whispers. "You like him, too."

My face burns and I tell her to shhh.

Miss Tina grabs our attention. "I've got a little story for you to help make sense of it all." She picks up some papers and asks us if we're ready. I settle back in my chair, alert, and ready to listen. I love stories. They remind me of when I was little and Dad used to read to me.

Long, long ago in the land that bobs in and out of view depending upon the sea mist, there was once a time when the fuzzy bag that each child was born with contained only Warm Fuzzies. The people had belief in their hearts; they believed that they could give and receive Warm Fuzzies freely, and their fuzzy bags would never be empty. They lived in perfect harmony, without a shred of fear in their hearts that they would run out of Warm Fuzzies and have none left for themselves. But through the ages some people's hearts were filled with disbelief and they became frightened that they would run out of Warm Fuzzies if they gave them away freely. They didn't realize that if they couldn't give Warm Fuzzies away to other people their fuzzy bags would be full of Cold Pricklies, for a fuzzy bag is never empty, it is always full of something.

One young woman called Neola, whose parents' fuzzy bags were so full of Cold Pricklies that she'd never learned what Warm Fuzzies were, felt very sad.

She felt so alone but bravely set off each morning trying to give from her fuzzy bag to the people she met. Yet each time she reached into her fuzzy bag, a Cold Pricklie would pounce upon the person in front of her and shrivel their sense of worth. Everyone she met eventually backed away from her with fear on their faces. It happened so often that Neola finally stopped going out and she felt as if she was a prisoner in her own home, alone with her fuzzy bag full of Cold Pricklies.

On the first of May the people of the village held a dance and, as it was her birthday, she decided to venture from her house. She wore her finest frock, and with anxiety in her heart she went to the dance. Bravely she joined in, dancing around the Maypole, her fuzzy bag bobbing about on her hip.

When the music stopped, she noticed that everyone reached into their fuzzy bags to share their

Warm Fuzzies. Lots of people gave her Warm Fuzzies, but she didn't know what to do with them, as her parents had never shown her. So, anxious to give something back, she reached into her fuzzy bag and gave away the only thing she had: Cold Pricklies. One by one the villagers backed away from her, and when she asked them to dance, they made excuses not to. By the end of the evening she stood alone, her fuzzy bag full to the brim with Cold Pricklies, and her heart was heavy and cold.

That night she sobbed and sobbed with loneliness, the Cold Pricklies in her fuzzy bag escaping and settling upon her shoulders, shrivelling her sense of worth. She was empty with despair, and in the darkness of the night she ran away, deciding that she would never speak to another living soul again. But as she traveled through the night, her loneliness grew more and more until she thought that she would die from the pain she felt.

She sat on a fallen tree trunk in the woods and sobbed, her cries echoing through the forest.

She was startled by a fox who crept up towards her with cunning, his fuzzy bag tied around his neck.

"Why are you crying?" he asked.

"When people share from their fuzzy bags they seem to laugh, yet when I share from my fuzzy bag, no one laughs, and no one wants to be around me."

Neola poured out her story to the cunning fox, and when she had finished he smiled slyly.

"I know just what you should do," he said, reaching into his fuzzy bag and pulling out a round fuzzy creature with eight wriggling tentacles.

Neola jumped back in alarm.

"What's that?" she cried.

"It's a Tepid Ticklie," the cunning fox replied, and as he spoke, it leaped upon Neola and began to tickle her.

She laughed until her sides hurt, and as the Tepid Ticklie jumped back into the fox's fuzzy bag, she felt better than she'd felt in a long time.

"What was that?" she asked again.

"It's a Tepid Ticklie. Everyone's fuzzy bag is filled with something, and if you are unable to give Warm Fuzzies, but realize that people won't like you if all you have to give are Cold Pricklies, then Tepid Ticklies trick people into believing that you have Warm Fuzzies in your fuzzy bag. Tepid Ticklies make you laugh and they allow you to give something to other people, yet they let you keep your Warm Fuzzies safe and hidden.

"Can I have some?" Neola asked, suddenly realizing that the reason no one wanted to be near her was because her fuzzy bag was full to the brim with Cold Pricklies.

"Of course," the cunning fox replied.

Neola tipped her fuzzy bag upside down and

hundreds of Cold Pricklies fell to the forest floor, where the cunning fox chased them away. She smiled as he filled her fuzzy bag with Tepid Ticklies, and with hope in her heart she hugged him and bade him goodbye.

The cunning fox chuckled to himself as he crept back to his den, for he had tricked Neola and given her the worst Cold Pricklie of all. He failed to tell her that Tepid Ticklies were loaded with sarcasm, which initially made people laugh but left them robbed of their sense of worth, and that Tepid Ticklies were really Cold Pricklies in disguise.

Neola set off towards the village, tired but happy, believing that she would be accepted by the villagers who shared their Warm Fuzzies freely. As she met them, she reached into her fuzzy bag and tossed a Tepid Ticklie at each person, and they smiled at her. By the time she reached her house, she felt happier than she had ever felt before and fell into bed exhausted.

Over the next few days Neola reveled in the fact that she was able to make people laugh and smile, and she finally began to feel as if the villagers liked her. But as the week came to an end, she became uneasy. She began to notice that when a Tepid Ticklie settled on the shoulders of those she gave them to, at first they would smile, and then confusion would flash across their faces before they started to back away from her, as they had in the past.

"What can be wrong?" she fretted to herself. "My Tepid Ticklies make me laugh and they make other people laugh, so why are people still backing away from me? I don't understand."

Over the next week Neola noticed that most of the villagers avoided her if they could, so she resorted to talking to the children, who each had trust in their eyes. She reached into her fuzzy bag and gave them a Tepid Ticklie, expecting them to laugh along with her, but she was shocked when one by one they pouted, frowning at her.

"Ouch, that hurt," one child said honestly.

"That's mean," said another.

"Why are you making fun of me?" yet another said, looking hurt.

Neola stuttered, not knowing what to say. She had no friends and she didn't want to chase away the only people who would speak to her.

"My Tepid Ticklies are supposed to make you laugh," she said with confusion on her face, but the little children didn't bother to answer her before they ran away.

She cried all the way home until she met a young man, idling by the roadside. She didn't dare give him a Tepid Ticklie for fear of him showing the same reaction as everyone else had, and so she began to walk past him.

"Hey," he called. "I thought everyone in this village gave from their fuzzy bags. How come you haven't given me something from your fuzzy bag? Give me something."

She looked at him and faltered for a moment. If he asked for what she had in her fuzzy bag then surely he wouldn't run from her, so slowly she opened her fuzzy bag and threw a Tepid Ticklie at him.

"Wow," he said, his eyes wide with wonder, "what is that? I've never seen such a thing. Can I have some for my fuzzy bag?"

So Neola gave him lots of Tepid Ticklies and soon his fuzzy bag was full of them. He walked along the road with Neola and threw a Tepid Ticklie onto her shoulders.

"Hey, do you want a drink?" he asked her.

"Yes," she said, her eyes alive and happy, thinking that he wanted to share with her.

"Well, get it yourself," he said, laughing.

The smile on her face faded and she suddenly felt cold and shivery.

He threw another Tepid Ticklie at her.

"I like your new haircut."

"Oh, thank you," she said, her face beginning to brighten again, but instantly her feelings were dashed.

"Did they cut it with a lawn mower?"

He threw her yet another Tepid Ticklie, which settled around her shoulders and began to tickle her.

"Knock, knock..."

"Who's there," she replied, starting to smile at the joke she knew was coming.

"Amanda."

"Amanda who?"

"Amanda your own business, you nosy busy-body."

Neola's face was crestfallen as the Tepid Ticklie changed from making her feel good to feeling shivery and hurt.

"Don't," she cried.

"What's the matter?" the young man asked, "It's a joke; can't you take a joke? What's wrong with you? You've got no sense of humor."

He threw yet another Tepid Ticklie at her, enjoying himself and being oblivious to her pain.

"I like your new dress." Again her spirits began to soar.

"If it rains you can use it as a tent."

As he laughed and laughed, something happened inside Neola. Suddenly she knew why all the villagers backed away from her when she gave them the Tepid Ticklies that the cunning fox had given her.

She ran from the young man and didn't stop running until she reached the safety of her home, and there, panting hard and too hurt to cry, she sat and thought about what was inside her fuzzy bag.

She realized that the cunning fox had tricked her, that the Tepid Ticklies were really Cold Prick-

lies in disguise, and although they initially made people smile, they ultimately hurt as much as Cold Pricklies did. No wonder all the villagers had backed away from her and left her alone.

She paced through her house, sleep evading her. She had liked the way she'd felt when the villagers smiled at her before they realized that her Tepid Ticklies were going to make them feel bad. She had never known the warm fuzzy feeling of sharing Warm Fuzzies, and yet she supposed that those initial feelings after a Tepid Ticklie settled upon your shoulders must be similar to the wonderful warm fuzzy feeling that Warm Fuzzies gave. She cried with regret and also with a little fear. She knew that, from that moment on, she was never going to give away Tepid Ticklies or Cold Pricklies, and that the only thing she wanted to give and receive was Warm Fuzzies. She never wanted to feel as bad as she had felt while walking home with the young man, whose fuzzy bag was now full of Tepid Ticklies.

As the sun began to rise, she knew that the only thing she could do to be rid of Tepid Ticklies and Cold Pricklies forever was to empty her fuzzy bag. She opened the window and shook it hard, watching all the Cold Pricklies and Tepid Ticklies scatter in the wind.

She felt afraid, mortally afraid, as she believed that her fuzzy bag was empty for the first time.

But she didn't know the truth, that a fuzzy bag is never empty, it's always full of Warm Fuzzies if you only believe that they are there.

"I am afraid," she said to herself, "but I would rather live with fear than spread Tepid Ticklies and Cold Pricklies that shrivel your sense of worth and cause you dreadful pain."

So with determination and understanding in her heart, she ventured out into the village as the sun rose. As she met everyone in the village, she smiled at them and they smiled back, and finally she realized that her fuzzy bag was full of Warm Fuzzies. Never had she felt such joy. Her heart was warm and soft, and laughter rested upon her lips as the villagers hugged her with trust in their eyes.

And so it didn't seem to matter in the end that her parents had failed to teach her about Warm Fuzzies, for she learned the truth herself. She learned that giving away Tepid Ticklies and Cold Pricklies meant that she would end up being alone and would never experience the joy of sharing with the other villagers. She learned that the only way to experience joy was to share only Warm Fuzzies with those people around her. She learned that her fuzzy bag would never run out of Warm Fuzzies, and that if she shared her Warm Fuzzies, she would never be alone again.

Chapter Eight

Miss Tina smiles as she puts the papers on the floor. "Do you understand?" she asks. "When you share Warm Fuzzies, people will want to be with you. If you don't know how to share them, and only give out Cold Pricklies or Tepid Ticklies (sarcasm), people won't want to be around you. You may come from a family that doesn't know how to give Warm Fuzzies, or they may be afraid to give them away for fear of 'letting down their guard,' or letting others get too close. Don't worry, because you can learn how to give Warm Fuzzies and then your fuzzy bags, your hearts, will always be full of them."

I sigh. I wish, I truly do, that I could share Warm Fuzzies with Lesley, just as the other twins at the convention do. I still don't feel hopeful, though, and although I'm glad to be away from her vicious tongue, I can't help but wish that she was here listening to this. Maybe then she would change.

Miss Tina tells us that we're finished for the morning and I follow the others to the living room, where I get a soda from the fridge in the corner of the room. Velvet tells me that she's going down to the beach to chill out, and I'm just about to follow her when Miss Tina calls me and says that I have a family session. I feel panicked but follow her anyway into a small room. It's empty and she tells me to sit next to her.

She sees the panic on my face and says, "Don't worry. It'll be okay. Hopefully your parents can sort things out."

I shake my head, feeling hopeless. The door opens and Mom, Dad and Lesley walk into the room. My heart starts racing and I feel sick. They sit.

Miss Tina thanks them for coming and her voice sounds far away. My head's spinning and I can't think straight. Mom looks angry and Dad looks concerned. Lesley smiles at me. Everything feels wrong.

Miss Tina turns to Mom and says, "Mom, you look angry. What are you feeling right now?"

Mom seems flustered to be confronted. "I've had to take time off work to be here. This has nothing to do with me. It's *his* fault," she spits, nodding towards Dad.

Lesley still smiles at me. I look away.

Miss Tina speaks sharply and I'm surprised. "Ma'am, we do not lay blame here, we only try to understand what's happened and how we can improve things for you all."

Mom looks affronted, but Dad looks relieved. I feel nervous. Mom isn't used to being spoken to like that.

"Divorce is difficult for everyone concerned," Miss Tina says, more gently, "and what we hope to achieve during our family sessions is to figure out what went wrong and how to build a new blended family, so that everyone feels that they have a valued place in the new family."

Mom makes a disparaging noise that tells us she's mad and doesn't want to listen.

"Lesley, what are your thoughts about your parents getting a divorce?"

Lesley smiles sweetly at Miss Tina and I want to shout out that she's faking. "I was surprised at the time," she says sensibly, "but I'm used to it now. I don't understand why Maizy can't accept that we are going to have a new mom and new brothers and sisters."

I want to claw her eyes out, and my heart races so badly that it's pounding in my chest. Mom looks furious.

"You aren't going to have a new mom. *I'm* your mother!" she snaps.

"That's quite right," Miss Tina says calmly, "but Dad's new wife will have a place in this new family too, and I understand that it'll take some time to get used to it. No one can take your place as the girls' mother."

Before Mom can object Miss Tina turns to Dad and says, "What are you feeling?" Lesley still smiles at me.

"I, I, um, it's been hard," he stutters.

"Hard, why?"

He falters for a moment as we look at him.

"It's been hard because I've tried to do the right thing."

"How so?" Miss Tina presses.

"I feel so guilty," he whispers. "I didn't mean for any of this to happen. It just did." He looks at me, and even though I feel swamped with my own feelings, I see anguish on his face. It shocks me and I want to hug him and tell him it'll be okay, but I don't. "I just want my girls to get along with each other, and with Carol's kids."

Something snaps inside me. I was getting along with Ronan just fine until Dad chose to run off with my boyfriend's mother and turn him into my brother. The injustice pours out of me as I tell them what I think, and all my pain lands on the floor in front of us, raw and messy. I don't care, though. It may be what Dad wanted but what about what *I* wanted? What Ronan wanted? I never had a say in what's happened to our family, and as I think it, I reluctantly recognize that Lesley and all of Carol's kids didn't have a say, either.

"I'm so sorry," Dad says, helplessly when my tirade comes to a tearful end.

Mom's voice slices through the room. "What about me? You put me through hell." She starts crying loudly, but Miss Tina stops her with one question.

"Why do you think your husband left you?"

My breath catches in my throat, and Mom's response seems to hover in the air. She all but spits at Miss Tina. "What? He left because of that whore."

Dad surprises me as he finally stands up to someone. "Carol is not a whore."

Miss Tina is very calm and addresses Mom. "No one just leaves their husband or wife, especially if they have children and a home together. Divorce is a painful business. It hurts everyone. Why would you do it unless there's a really good reason?"

If Mom were a kettle she'd be boiling great billows of scalding stream. She can't answer Miss Tina's question.

"Dad, why did you leave?" Miss Tina presses, and I hold my breath waiting to see if he will answer and if he's braver than Mom.

"Because I couldn't stand her nagging me anymore, or putting me down. I've worked hard to give her and the twins everything they needed, but nothing I did was ever enough. I couldn't stand the drama either," he adds.

"The drama?" Miss Tina asks. "What do you mean by that?"

Dad looks really uncomfortable but he carries on. "I don't know. It was as if she was bored if everything was going okay. I'd feel content but she'd find a reason to pick a fight."

"How dare you say that," Mom explodes. "I worked just as hard as you did, and *I* wasn't unfaithful."

I shake my head, losing her point. Dad looks confused and I see helplessness in his eyes.

I speak out. "Mom, you did the same as Dad. You had sex with Leo when you were still married to Dad." He shoots me a grateful look, which I ignore because I'm not rescuing him. All I care about is my family being truthful in the same way I've experienced since being at Beach Haven. My family's full of lies and I'm tired of it. Mom flashes me a look that says she hates me.

Miss Tina doesn't miss it and again speaks sharply. "Ma'am, we're not here to lay blame, only to understand. What do you think your husband means by saying that he felt you were bored and deliberately picked fights?"

It seems ages before Mom speaks, but I guess it's only a few seconds. She glances towards Dad and says, "Well, you were boring."

"So you picked fights with him to relieve your boredom?" Miss Tina asks.

Dad turns to look at Mom and we wait for her to answer. Her face is very red. I feel scared at the confrontation in the room. I hate it. She bursts into tears.

"How could you leave us?" she sobs. "We've been together forever."

Dad looks like he's in pain. "I couldn't take anymore," he says, shrugging.

"Why didn't you say?" Mom asks, as her nose runs and Miss Tina hands her a box of tissues.

Dad shrugs again and says, "There was no talking to you. You shouted me down every time I tried to talk to you. You put me down all the time." His thoughts hang in the air, settling on us like flurries of icy snowflakes.

No one says anything and I look towards Miss Tina, praying that she'll make things right, but she sits still, saying nothing. My stomach is sick and I need the bathroom. I ask to be excused and return minutes later to find them all still sitting around the room with their own discomfort in their laps. I sit down.

Miss Tina turns towards me and says, "We waited for you, Maizy. We won't talk about things without you here." She talks to us all and no one in particular. "It's so sad that people finally get to talk honestly after they've split up or divorced. Perhaps it all could have been avoided if you'd been able to be this honest earlier, or perhaps not. We'll never know, and really it doesn't matter because what's done is done. I know that may sound harsh, but what we're faced with now is that you, Dad, are marrying someone else and there's a baby on the way, right?"

Dad nods miserably.

"What we need to do is move on. How can we fix this family so that each of you feel that you belong, and each of you feel respected?" Miss Tina asks, forcing Mom and Dad to think rather than blame each other. Lesley still smiles at me but I look away.

Miss Tina continues and we look towards her for guidance. I know I feel lost and I imagine Mom and Dad do, too. They look miserable.

"Dad, what would you like to say to your ex-wife?"

Dad looks mortified, but when Miss Tina nods at him in encouragement, he turns towards Mom and says, very slowly as if he's thinking out loud, "I'm *so* sorry. I wish we'd gone to some kind of counseling before all this happened. I've always loved you, but I just couldn't take the nagging anymore. I really felt as if you hated me. I couldn't cope." Then he glances between me and Lesley and says, "I'm really sorry, girls. I didn't mean to hurt you. I love you. I'm sorry." Tears pour down my face as I hear the pain in his voice.

A fresh sob bursts from Mom and she grabs a handful of tissues, blowing her nose noisily. "I'm sorry," she sobs. "I didn't realize I was being so mean. I wish you'd said," she adds.

Dad looks really bad and Miss Tina rescues him by saying to Mom, "You should have known. You are responsible for your own behavior, no one else."

Mom sobs again and speaks brokenly, "I'm sorry. I'm sorry. I wish I could turn the clock back."

Miss Tina speaks out. "Unfortunately you can't do that, because there's a baby on the way, and this baby didn't ask to be born, just as none of your seven children asked for all of this to happen. What you have to do is to move forward with a new understanding of each other, a new respect , so that all the children in this blended family feel as if they belong and are valued. And that means that all four of you, Mom, Dad, step-mom and Leo, model the kind of behavior you want to see in your children—respect and tolerance."

Miss Tina turns to me and says, "Maizy, I know things have been hard for you since your dad left, but what do you want to happen? What can your parents do to make things right for you?"

Everything inside me wants to shout, "Come back, Dad. Leave Carol, come home where you belong, and then I can be with Ronan again," but as I think it, I know it's an impossible dream.

Everyone looks at me and Lesley's still smiling. An image of a macabre clown pops into my head and I try to ignore her. My thoughts are swirling around my head like water down a drain and I struggle to contain them.

"I do accept what's happened," I find my voice. "I don't like it, Dad, and I wish you'd come home, but I know that won't happen." I pause, trying to pick my words carefully. "I think that all I want is for you to stand up for yourself and for us, for me."

I see him flinch and I know I've hit a nerve.

"I just want you to stand up for me when Lesley hurts me."

Lesley takes a sharp intake of breath in righteous indignation, glancing between Mom and Dad, obviously expecting them to tell me to shut up. They don't and Lesley watches with every nerve alive, waiting. I try to ignore her, and even though I feel really sick and need the bathroom again, I press on. "I want you to believe me when I say that I've done nothing to Millie." The injustice of it all floods over me again and tears fill my eyes. "How could you believe that I would blacken Millie's eye? Dad, you know I couldn't do that. I wouldn't. I don't like her, I'll admit, but that's because she's so mean to me and tries to get me into trouble."

Miss Tina turns towards Lesley and asks her what she thinks about it all. She astounds me by saying, "I don't know why Dad would believe Millie. She's always lying."

I gape at her, unable to believe what I'm hearing. I suddenly wonder if I'm going crazy. I've told everyone at Beach Haven that my sister's hateful, yet here she is being nice. I don't get it. Dad and Mom look confused, too. Lesley shrugs her shoulders slowly in an act of defiance.

"What?" she asks innocently. "You asked me what I think." Either Lesley's playing a sick game or I've gone completely crazy.

Miss Tina seems to ignore Lesley and speaks directly to Mom and Dad. She praises them for being honest and tells them that this isn't the end of their relationship, it's just the beginning of a new, different one, one that'll take some adjusting to, but one that'll be okay if they all work at it.

I sense from Miss Tina's tone of voice that the family session is nearly over and I'm relieved. She stands, and so do I. I want to join Velvet and the other kids on the beach. In fact, I long to be as far away from this room as possible. Being on the beach and letting the waves lap against my ankles and feeling the sun beating down on my shoulders seems like heaven compared to the heaviness in this room. Lesley still smiles at me. What's going on?

As Miss Tina opens the door, Lesley turns to me and says. "Maizy, we're twins. You're my sister, my *real* sister. I need to a car. I helped take care of the cat, as well."

I don't know what she's talking about, but Mom enlightens me.

"Oh, Maizy, I forgot to tell you. Mrs. White left you lots of money in her will so that you can go to college."

"What?" I say, stunned.

Miss Tina stands in the doorway as Mom explains. "She left her house to her daughter but everything else she left to you. She said that she loved you and was indebted to you for all the years that you kept her company and took care of Sooty." Mom has tears in her eyes. "I'm proud of you, Maizy. I know I don't tell you often enough, but I am."

Lesley objects. Her voice is whiny. "But Mom, I took turns in taking care of the cat. It's not fair."

She can't even say Sooty's name. I look at her and now I understand the game she's been playing—she wants Mrs. White's money and if that means having to be nice to me, that's what she'll do. Anger flashes through me and I shake my head.

"You tried to set fire to Sooty's tail," I say, trying to control myself.

"No, I didn't. That's a lie. You were just trying to get me into trouble," Lesley spits at me, all semblance of the fixed smile lost on her face. I see the hatred I knew was lurking there all the time.

I feel afraid and look at Miss Tina, willing her to rescue me from the sudden burst of hatred that has exploded into the room.

Miss Tina orders us to sit down again and shuts the door.

"I see that we haven't finished truly expressing how we feel," she says knowingly. "Lesley, I don't think you've been as honest as your mom and dad have been. Perhaps you'd like to say what's really on your mind." Lesley glares at her dangerously, which Miss Tina ignores.

"Go on," Miss Tina urges. "Let's hear it."

Lesley falters and turns towards Dad. "Dad, you know I used to take care of the cat. Well, Maizy lied about me. I didn't do anything to it."

I open my mouth to object but Miss Tina holds her hand out to silence me. My palms are sweating and my heart's racing.

Dad shakes his head. He doesn't know what to say and I fear he's going to back down under Lesley's badgering of him, but he shrugs. "Mrs. White made a choice. She chose Maizy to help her. I don't know what to say," he adds.

"But it's not fair," Lesley continues to whine. "Maizy lied about me and now *she* gets the money."

"It's Mrs. White's choice," Dad says again.

Lesley's voice moves up a notch as she protests even louder. "But that's not fair. She should share it with me. It's only fair." Lesley looks at me and her face is contorted with hatred. "You scheming, con-niving bitch," she spits at me, all pretense gone. "I hate you."

Miss Tina's voice is sharper than I've ever heard it. "Stop it! That's enough!" It slices through the hatred hanging in the air. Mom and Dad look morti-fied and ashamed. I feel sick.

I expect Miss Tina to lecture her, but she surprises me by turning away from Lesley and facing me. Her voice is calm and sweet. "Maizy, this is a time for you to use the things you've learned in group."

Instantly, my thoughts fall into place. I know what she's getting at.

"She just gave me a Cold Pricklie," I cry, "but I don't have to take it. I can dodge it. It belongs to her, not me. I can't change her, I can only change the way I respond to her. I can give her Warm Fuzzies and hope that she'll behave differently," I repeat, trying to remember everything I've been taught.

Miss Tina beams at me as Mom, Dad and Lesley sit there dumbfounded.

Lesley's the first to recover. "Dad, tell her. Tell her she has to share the money with me. I need a car, and you can't afford one," then her face twists with sarcasm, "now that you've got a new baby coming."

I glance at Miss Tina and there's a flicker of a smile on her face that eggs me on. "And that was a Tepid Ticklie, which is really a Cold Pricklie in dis-guise," I say. "They hurt as much as Cold Pricklies do, but I don't have to catch them. I can give Warm Fuzzies," I repeat, making it clear in my head and warding off Lesley's hatred with logic.

With a massive effort I think of something nice to

say. "Lesley, I'm really sorry that Mrs. White didn't want you to come over or to take care of Sooty."

Lesley looks shaken, confused, and then all pretense flies out of the window. "F**k you," she cusses, and gets up to leave. She slams the door behind her.

Mom and Dad look really embarrassed. I feel stunned, but glad that the hatred is out in the open at last. Dad shakes his head and blames himself.

"I should have been stronger with her. Maizy was always so easy to deal with and Lesley, so difficult. It was easier to give in to her." He looks at me, crushed, with guilt on his face. "I'm so sorry, Maizy, I should have been stronger and fought in your corner more."

Mom speaks out. "Me too. I'm sorry." She turns to Dad—it's weird that they're talking, not yelling. "It's not just you that hasn't been strong with Lesley. I haven't either." She turns to Miss Tina and says, "She's so difficult, y'know. Always has been." Then Mom turns to me and her voice cracks. "Baby, I'm so sorry. When you and Lesley argued, I couldn't cope with it. I just wanted it to stop."

"You sent me to my room," I say dully. "Every time."

Miss Tina is intent on forcing us to be honest with each other. "And that made you feel...?"

"Invisible, picked on, unloved..." I can't think of anything else, but I think I've covered it.

Mom starts to cry again and Dad puts his arm around her. They hold each other and I feel as if I'm a spectator watching a sad love story. I want to cry, too. Their closeness feeds into my dreams that they'll get back together. Miss Tina glances at me and there's a smile on her face.

I sit there watching as Dad comforts Mom, and they whisper their regret, vowing to be stronger in the future. Their words fill me with hope, but a small voice inside me knows that their relationship has changed, and they'll never get back together. Suddenly I'm okay with it. As I watch them being as honest as the kids are in group, I feel hope. What does it matter if they're married to other people if they can be this honest and caring towards each other? I just need everyone to stop fighting, and I need to know that my parents still care about each other, and I can see that they do.

I don't say anything and neither does Miss Tina. We just watch. My head is swimming. Something really major has happened in this room. I've never seen my mom and dad be this affectionate. I swallow hard, blinking back my tears.

The door bursts open and Lesley fills the space.

"We need to go home," she demands. "Mark is picking me up in an hour."

Mark? I'm surprised when it doesn't hurt me. I remember his words, "I'll go with anyone who'll give me what I want." I look at Lesley standing in the doorway while Mom and Dad express their regret and their ongoing but changing love for each other, and I feel defeated. I don't know how to reach my twin. I remember everything Miss Tina and Miss Cassie have taught me and I try to apply it to this situation. I refuse to give Lesley any Cold Pricklies, even though she gives them to me and invites me to give them back. I've tried to give her a Warm Fuzzie but she dodged it and it fell at her feet. She chose not to take it.

Miss Tina says, "We're not done yet. Come and have a seat."

Lesley stands in the doorway, scanning the room, and she's obviously mad because she scowls at Mom and Dad when she sees them hugging. She then cusses at me, saying I'll be sorry, before turning around and slamming the door loudly.

Mom pulls away from Dad and faces Miss Tina. "What should I do?" she asks, with hopelessness hanging from her like a wild vine strangling a tree.

Miss Tina is thoughtful for a moment, and then sets us all free.

"You've been good parents. You've done your best and that's all we can ask for. Lesley and Maizy are old enough to be responsible for their own behavior. They are not children anymore. All parents make mistakes—there's no rule book that tells us how to be a parent. I can see that you are both loving parents. Do not blame yourselves. Lesley has learned that she can get what she wants by causing havoc in your family. You have all been subject to this, not just Maizy."

"But what can we do?" Mom asks again, and I can't believe how gentle her voice has become. I've never known her to be like this. A thought flashes through my mind that perhaps I don't know her at all. Suddenly I want to hug her, but I sit still, wrestling with my feelings, waiting for her to speak. "I love my girls," she says. "I know they're as different as night and day, but they're my babies, my twins. I don't understand why they can't get along."

I don't either. It has confused me since I was old enough to think.

Miss Tina holds our attention. "Y'know, there is a massive argument among scholars the world over that personality is the product of our genes, yet others argue that our personalities are a product of our upbringing, how we raise our kids. No one can say for sure which is more important." She leans forward, intent on helping us all understand. "It would be too easy to blame our behavior on our genes, but every human being has free will. Free will means that we all have a choice as to how to behave. Lesley doesn't have to be mean, but she chooses to because she's learned that being mean and demanding will get her what she wants."

I cringe. Miss Tina amazes me. Sometimes she's gentle, sweet and funny, but other times she's like a pit-bull terrier. I feel safe around her, but occasionally she fills me with dread, and now is one of those times.

A sob escapes Mom. "It's my fault. I was too tired. Their fights were so vicious. I didn't understand. Every year we'd go to the twin convention and I'd see little kids who were so attuned to each other that they'd know what the other was thinking. It forced me to see that my girls weren't like that. I hated it. It made me feel like a failure as a mother."

Dad chips in as he looks at Mom. "I felt that, too. I felt like a failure as a father." He falls silent for a moment and the only sound in the room is Mom sniffing. Then he frowns and looks at Miss Tina and says, "What's a Warm Fuzzie and a Cold Pricklie? And what's a Tepid... what?"

"A Tepid Ticklie," Miss Tina corrects. "Sir, I'm going to give you some homework to do. All four of you, Carol and Leo too, are to read the papers about Warm Fuzzies, Cold Pricklies and Tepid Ticklies, and I want you to come to the next family session with a complete understanding of them so that you can really communicate with Maizy. She's learned this stuff and that means that she knows more than you do. You need to learn."

I'm blown away by Miss Tina's strength. It seems like she doesn't care if she makes my parents mad; all she seems to care about is teaching adults the same stuff she teaches us so that we can communicate properly.

Miss Tina stands up and she opens the door again. Mom and Dad shake her hand and assure her that they'll be here the same time next week to work on our problems.

Miss Tina floors me by saying to Mom and Dad, "I'd like you to bring Leo and Carol, and your step-children, next week so that we can include them and really get this blended family working."

I remain quiet. I don't want any of them to come here. Beach Haven has become my sanctuary, a place where I don't have to defend myself or suffer pain. I can speak honestly here, and everything I say will be accepted, even if it isn't liked. I don't want anyone to ruin that. It's been bad enough having Lesley here today, but Millie will be worse, I just know it. I don't want them here. This place is amazing and it's my lifeline. I don't want to share it with people who hate me.

I see irritation flash across Mom's face, and I know she doesn't want to be in the same room as Carol, and Miss Tina sees it too.

"It's the only way," Miss Tina says calmly, and Mom nods reluctantly.

Chapter Nine

I watch Mom and Dad through the window as they head towards the car. Lesley's leaning against it and, as Mom stands by the locked door when Dad gets in, Lesley flares up at her. I can't hear what they're saying but I get what's happening. Mom thrusts her face into Lesley's and then she wags her finger at her. Lesley backs away in surprise.

Miss Tina stands behind me and watches. I look at her, wondering what she's thinking.

"Well, good for her," she says smiling. "I think your mom has just taken a stand against Lesley. Good job."

I grin. I wish I could hear what they're saying. Mom stands with her feet apart and I know she means business. Lesley gets into the car and Mom slams the door behind her.

Miss Tina laughs and says, "Okay, so Mom's now taking charge but we still need to work on her Cold Pricklies."

I laugh too. Miss Tina hugs me and tells me that I was awesome in the family session and had faced my fears in order to be honest. She tells me to go and find the others on the beach. I all but run out of the building; my heart feels light.

"Hey, girl," Velvet calls, as she sees me run over the grassy ridge that separates Beach Haven from the beach. I'm panting by the time I flop down on the sand next to her and the others.

"How did it go?" Velvet asks.

"Yeah, how was it? My first one was rocky," Lexi says.

The guys all look towards me. I smile, feeling suddenly light and happy.

"It was awful but great," I say, laughing. "My parents were better than I expected they'd be, but my sister was her awful self. She walked out. Hey, I can't believe it, but my neighbor who died left me a load of money for college. My sister's really mad. She tried to manipulate Mom and Dad into giving her half because she wants a car."

"What did they say?" Marcus asks.

"Dad said it was my neighbor's choice and that's when she walked out."

"She didn't get her own way, then?" Velvet asks, grinning.

"Not this time."

We goof around on the sand and I feel lighter inside than I have since Christmas. The others tell me about their family sessions, how sometimes they're great and other times things don't work out. I try not to let my apprehension about my next session bring me down.

After lunch we sit in the Group Room again and a man sits next to Miss Tina.

"Hi, Maizy," he says. "I'm Ken. I'm one of the counselors here. I've been away on vacation. Nice to meet you."

"He's cool," Velvet whispers to me.

Miss Tina begins to talk and everyone gets quiet. "Okay, let's recap quickly to let Ken know what we're up to. Every human from the moment of birth to the moment of death seeks Strokes, and any Stroke is better than no Stroke. We've learned that if you continually give out negative Strokes—Cold Pricklies or Tepid Ticklies—people won't want to be around you and they'll probably leave. You'll end up alone like poor Neola."

She jumps up and walks to the flipchart. "Did any of you notice?" she asks.

I look around the room to see if anyone knows what she's talking about. They look as confused as I am. She writes Neola on the page and then starts picking out the letters and writes them below. The word spells, "alone."

"Oh," several of the kids say together.

"Cool," Lexi says.

Miss Tina sits down again and begins talking.

"Ken, we also learned that everyone has a choice as to how to respond to someone who gives out positive or negative Strokes. Human beings have the capacity to be kind or hateful, and they have the free will to choose which way they behave. You may choose to give out Cold Pricklies or Tepid Ticklies, especially if you've learned that you can get your own way by being mean, and you may even like the power you think it gives you over other people. You may not want to change, but the most important reason why you need to change is this. In the future most of you will become parents. Now, if all you have in your fuzzy bags, your hearts, are Cold Pricklies, that's all you'll be able to give to your children, and you'll cause them pain."

Miss Tina looks around the room and she's deadly serious. "There's not one of you in this room who doesn't know what it feels like to be hurt." Several of the kids nod. "Would you want your child to go through the same pain you have? Would you?"

Everyone says no. I know that I couldn't bear any child of mine to hurt as badly as I have under the relentless barrage of Cold Pricklies from Lesley over the years. When I'm a mom, I'm going to do things very differently, that's for sure.

"So even though change is difficult, and it's easy to slip back into your old ways, particularly when you're stressed," Miss Tina continues, "it's impor- tant to practice giving Warm Fuzzies and dodging

Cold Pricklies and Tepid Ticklies, if only for that reason."

"Yeah, but all of my family gives out Tepid Ticklies, even my grandparents," Rocky says. "They don't see anything wrong in it."

"But you don't have to," Miss Tina answers him. "Can you see that your parents learned how to interact from their own parents. And they obviously weren't comfortable giving out Warm Fuzzies, so, as any Stroke is better than no Stroke, they swapped Tepid Ticklies. You have the opportunity to change how your family interacts. You can break the cycle. Isn't that exciting?" she asks animatedly.

"I think it's exciting," I say. "And I'm definitely going to make sure I don't have anything else in my fuzzy bag other than Warm Fuzzies. I'd hate my children to feel the way I do."

Miss Tina beams at me. "Maizy, I was so proud of you this morning. Guys, everything Maizy has told you about her sister is true. I really do believe that you have asked that special question of yourself." Ken looks blank. "The 'What did *I* do?' question," she explains. He nods.

"Can I tell the others what happened?" she asks me. I nod. "Maizy's sister Lesley threw several Cold Pricklies at Maizy, which she carefully and deliberately dodged. I was *so* proud."

"It was hard," I say. "I felt really angry, and it would have been easy to retaliate and lob a Cold

Pricklie back at her. And I'm not saying I didn't want to either, but I remembered that I had a choice." I grin at the kids looking at me. "I had a picture of us all lobbing blue beanbags at each other and dodging them, so I focused on that image and mentally dodged her insults. It worked. She got mad and left."

Everyone starts clapping and I feel like a million dollars. A thought dawns on me. "Hey, isn't that how you can deal with bullies at school? If you can dodge their insults and ignore them, they'll get fed up and pick on someone else who will react."

"Good point," Miss Tina says.

"But I don't get why people would want to swap anything other than Warm Fuzzies," Marion says. "Why hurt other people?"

"That's a good question," Miss Tina says. "Why d'you think they do?" She looks around the room.

Rocky says, "Because some people are aggressive."

Alfie suggests. "Because some people think they're better than others."

I'm thinking of Lesley and Mrs. White's will. "I think it's because people want what others have."

"Yeah, because they're greedy," Velvet chips in.

"But they wouldn't do these things if they had a conscience, would they?" Marion asks.

"Ah," Miss Tina cries. "Now we've found the truth. Oh, how smart you all are. A conscience is what separates us from the animals. Animals are driven by the need to feed and mate, and they don't have the same thought processes as humans do that would allow them to consider their actions right or wrong. Human beings do. So that gives us a dilemma. We can behave as animals and allow ourselves to be driven by the urges inside us—lust, greed, gluttony and the other seven deadly sins—or we can think and make choices based on our consciences."

Ken adds. "And the way we develop a conscience depends on how we're brought up in our families. If you do something wrong, and we all do, and you're expected to make amends for it, you'll develop a conscience."

I'm thinking quickly as they teach us. Something's bothering me, so I speak up. "I think that I've got a conscience because, even though I've given out Cold Pricklies in the past, I've always felt bad about it. But I don't think that Lesley has one, because it doesn't seem to bother her at all when she hurts people—not just me, but she hurts Mom and Dad and the kids at school, too."

I sit up in my chair and I can feel myself charged with the thoughts that spring into my mind. "But how can that be, when she and I are identical twins? We're the same and yet we're not."

Miss Tina beams at me. "Oh, Maizy, you precious child. Do you know what you've just done? You've just spelled it out for all of us. You and Lesley are identical twins. That means that you share the same genes, you are the same flesh, but you show us that each person has a choice as to how to be—whether to be good or evil. That's how it is for all mankind; we have a choice as to how we behave."

Ken pipes up. "That's why it's a good thing to have some kind of spiritual belief, because without some sort of 'guidance' it would be easy to be tempted by the drives that are in all of us." A couple of the kids balk, but he tries to explain himself. "I've got a little baby. She's a cutie, but you can see in her the drives that we are all born with. She wants what she wants when she wants it. It's my job, as her father, to help her learn to control those drives, and teach her to wait and consider other people. That's how she'll develop a conscience. If I don't help her do that, she'll grow up wanting what she wants when she wants it, and she won't care about who's in her way."

I get it, and I vow to myself that I'm going to try harder to control myself more. I'm going to be on constant guard duty, because I refuse to give out Cold Pricklies and hurt people, even if they try to hurt me. I'm better than that.

Marion sounds frustrated. "But I still don't get why people would choose to seek Cold Pricklies instead of Warm Fuzzies."

Miss Tina speaks directly to her. "Remember that

any Stroke is better than no Stroke. If parents don't know how to give Warm Fuzzies because they've never been shown, they'll give Cold Pricklies. There's never nothing in your fuzzy bag. Your heart always has something in it. Human beings seek contact with others, it's part of the human condition. From the very moment of conception—you know what that means, egg and sperm joining—the developing human is in contact with another. First, its mother and after its birth, others. Human beings fear aloneness."

I frown and so do several of the other kids.

"I don't mean being alone. At times that's great; we all need our own space. I mean the sense that beyond ourselves there's nothing out there. It taps into our subconscious and makes us very afraid. This feeling of fear is the root of why people seek Cold Pricklies when they can't find any Warm Fuzzies. Any Stroke is better than no Stroke, remember?"

She looks around to see if we understand. I think I do.

"If you think about how life is for an unborn baby, it must be heaven. They're held firmly, feel secure, are warm and never hungry. They are continually 'stroked' by the sensation of their mother's uterus. They never feel alone, ever. Yet from the moment of birth until the moment of death, they will never experience the same degree of intimacy as they felt inside their mother's womb. This need for intimacy is what drives us to stay connected to other people—it softens the blow. It helps take the edge off the aloneness that we feel subconsciously."

She takes a sip of water from a glass on the table behind her. She sounds excited as if she's made a great discovery.

"Are you all with me?" she asks, and most of us say we are. I am. I'm fascinated. "If you can't share Warm Fuzzies to help stay connected to other humans, then you'll take the only other option left to you. You'll seek Cold Pricklies, even though they'll make you feel bad in the end."

She shakes her head and says, "Man, that's so awful. It hurts my heart to know that some people think they can't find any Warm Fuzzies and are too 'closed' to try a new way of behaving."

"Closed?" Lexi asks.

"Scared to try new ways of behaving," Miss Tina clarifies.

"Scared?" Lexi challenges.

"Oh, I know what she means," I pipe up. "I was scared to try to give Warm Fuzzies to Lesley this morning."

"Yes, but you tried. You're learning a new way of interacting with other people," Miss Tina says. "You are not scared of trying new ways of behaving."

A smile spreads across my face and I feel great.

Ken takes over. "So those people who are too scared to get close to other people—because that's what happens when you share Warm Fuzzies, you get close, you become intimate and—I'm not talking about sex—opt to share Cold Pricklies, and that means drama, and lots of it."

Oh, I know drama. Our house is a stage and we're the main players. Several of the kids groan, saying that they know what he means.

Ken stands up and walks to the flipchart. He starts to draw a triangle and at the top corner he writes, "Persecutor," and at the lower right-hand corner he writes "Rescuer," and finally at the left-hand corner he writes, "Victim."

"When people don't know how to be truly intimate, and what am I not talking about?" he asks, making sure we're still awake.

"Sex," everyone answers.

He grins at us. "Good job. You're all paying attention. When people don't know how to be truly intimate, they play mind games. These games allow people to swap lots of Cold Pricklies, which help them to fight their fear of aloneness but basically stop them from ever achieving true intimacy, and what am I *not* talking about?" he quips.

"Sex," we all chant.

"Good job," he praises, smiling at us, giving us a Warm Fuzzie. "You're listening. I'm impressed."

We laugh.

"Remember, we're driven to stay connected to other people, and how we do that depends on whether our families swap Warm Fuzzies or Cold Pricklies."

Most of the kids call out that their families only swap Cold Pricklies. A couple of the kids say that the warmest thing they've ever experienced was a Tepid Ticklie, and I see Miss Tina and Ken glance at each other and share a look of sadness between them.

"What we're going to look at now," Ken says, "is the drama that's involved in two people who share Cold Pricklies. You've all heard of mind games?"

Everyone says yes. It's a term that's batted around a lot at school when kids don't understand their boyfriend's behavior, and they feel manipulated or conned in some way. For me, it's not a boyfriend that plays mind games—Ronan never did—it's Lesley. But as I think it, I check myself. It's not only Lesley, it's Carol and Millie, too. I feel conned by them all, but not by Mom. I feel used and ignored, but not conned. I listen intently.

"Well, this diagram," Ken says, pointing to his triangle, "will show you the 'moves' people make when they play mind games. And why do people play mind games?" he quizzes us.

Silence hangs over us for a moment and then Velvet blurts out, "Of course," she tells herself, "people play mind games because they don't know how to be intimate." There's a grin on her face as she stares at Ken. "And I don't mean..."

She looks pointedly around the room and the kids crack up, saying, "Sex."

"Smart mouth," Ken plays with her.

"I'm listening to you, okay?"

Ken grins at her. I love this. I love being here, where everyone is valued. You can say what you like, there's no hiding place, but anything you say is okay. I've never known anything like it and right now I don't ever want to leave. I glance at Velvet and she's grinning. I laugh softly to myself.

"Okay, so this is how mind games work, and it's easy to recognize a mind game once you learn the moves. And the point is that you can step away from mind games once you recognize that you've become hooked into one. However, people who depend on these types of negative Strokes become expert at playing the moves, so you need to be on guard."

He points to the diagram. "You can see that there are three main positions on this drama triangle. It's called that because the moves cause drama, and there are three positions that people typically find themselves in: persecutor, rescuer or victim."

Everyone's very quiet.

"You can tell if you've been hooked into a mind game if you are in one of these positions on this triangle, and suddenly without warning you find yourself in another position, and feel confused or conned." Ken holds up his hand and says, "Hang in there with me, guys, it'll be clear in a minute."

I do as he asks, curious to see how this works.

"People who play mind games do so for a reason. Remember, it's so much better to swap Warm Fuzzies and be intimate with another human being." He grins and holds up his hand to silence us as we all get ready to chant the word "sex" again when we hear the word intimate.

"People who play mind games are scared of getting too close to other people. Perhaps they've been hurt before and don't know how to keep themselves safe. There are many reasons why people put up barriers and fail to share Warm Fuzzies that lead to closeness. You need to truly *know* yourself to become close to another person, and that means taking responsibility for the negative things about yourself. It takes insight. If people don't truly know themselves, in order to feel connected in some way to others to get rid of their fear of aloneness, they play mind games. Mind games prevent people from being truly intimate but they provide masses of Strokes, Cold Pricklies and Tepid Ticklies, which make people feel connected to other human beings."

He glances around the room to see if we're concentrating.

"The three main positions in the *game* are persecutor, rescuer and victim, and the purpose of the mind game is to generate drama, and to swap Strokes without letting down your defenses so that you become uncomfortably close to others."

"It all sounds like too much hard work," Alfie says. "Why would anyone bother?"

"Because mind games produce masses and masses of Strokes," Ken says patiently, "even though deep down they'll make you feel bad. People get used to feeling bad."

"It sounds dumb to me," Scott says. "I hate drama. There's so much of it in my house."

"I'm sorry," Ken says. "There was in my home, too. I know how it feels."

Miss Tina stands up and Ken says, "We're going to role play, okay? You figure out which position we're in at any given time. All the time we stay in one position, it's not a mind game. It only becomes a mind game when we switch positions. Watch and listen!"

Ken seems to turn into someone else before our eyes. He seems to shrink.

"I've tried really hard to please you, to get you everything you want," he whines at Miss Tina.

He turns towards us and asks what position he's in. I look at the options—persecutor, rescuer or victim.

"Victim," I say, and others agree with me. Ken tells me I'm right.

"Well, it's just not good enough," Miss Tina snaps. "I work two jobs to put food on the table. You need to get it together."

Miss Tina asks us what position she's in. Her tone

of voice is harsh and I'm reminded of my mom. Their behavior is exactly like my mom and dad.

I call out again, "Persecutor." Miss Tina nods.

Ken turns to us and says, "I try harder than ever to please her. I wear myself out."

Miss Tina says, "And I pick on him more and more for not being good enough."

"Until one day I meet someone else, and I go off with her," Ken says. "And this is what I say. 'I'm sick of your nagging. It's over.'"

He looks at us and asks what position he's in. *Persecutor,* I think. Lexi calls out first. She's right.

Miss Tina pretends to sob. "He's left me," she cries. A giggle seeps out of me as she sobs dramatically.

"And what position is she in?" Ken asks, while Miss Tina goes overboard and gets louder.

"Victim," several kids call out.

"Can you see that they ended up in different positions than the ones they started out in? That means that both of them were hooked into a mind game. They swapped lots of Cold Pricklies, experienced loads of drama, and avoided being close to each other, but stayed connected even though it hurt," Ken explains.

"That's how it was for my mom and dad," I cry. "Dad did everything for Mom but it was never enough, so he had an affair. Does that mean they were playing mind games?"

Miss Tina looks at me and challenges me. "Did they swap Warm Fuzzies that would allow them to be close, or did they swap Cold Pricklies?"

The answer is obvious to me, and I feel heavy-hearted as I say, "They swapped Cold Pricklies all the time."

"I think that if they swapped Cold Pricklies and they ended up in a different position on the drama triangle, you can safely say they were hooked into mind games," Ken says kindly, like he wants to soften the revelation.

I feel sad. If Mom and Dad had known this stuff, maybe they'd have made an effort to change, so that they wouldn't have allowed themselves to get hooked into mind games.

"But why?" I ask. "Why would they behave that way when they know it would ruin things?" It doesn't make any sense to me.

"Because they didn't believe that they could give and receive Warm Fuzzies," Miss Tina says.

"Let's look at another example," Ken says brightly.

I shake my head, trying to get rid of my sadness.

Miss Tina's face is downcast, and she looks anxious. "Oh Ken, I'm so worried. I've spent all weekend working on my assignment and it has to be handed in tomorrow. My kid's sick and I've been up all night. I can't think straight."

Ken faces Miss Tina and says, "Oh, I'm so sorry. What can I do to help? I know you're having a hard time at the moment." He faces us and asks what position he's in.

He's rescuing her. Velvet beats me and answers first. Ken says, "Good job."

"I'm used to people helping me," Miss Tina says to us. "When I play dumb, people come to my rescue and I get what I want."

"I'm used to being needed," Ken continues. "It's how I get my Strokes."

Miss Tina slips into role again and whines, "Oh, I'd be so grateful if you'd check my assignment for me and change what needs changing." Ken looks at us and asks, "What position is Miss Tina in right now?"

I look at the options again: persecutor, rescuer and victim.

"Still in victim," I say and others agree with me. Ken tells me I'm right.

Ken says, "And I'd gladly do her assignment because I want her to need me. I work on her assignment all night and only have a little time to finish my own. When she gets a higher mark than me, I get angry, and say, 'Well, that's the last time I help you.'"

He looks at us and asks, "What position am I in?"

"Persecutor," we all say together.

He beams at us, nods his head, and says, "You guys are great."

Miss Tina says, "I can remember a time at work years ago when I felt really irritated with my co-worker and I couldn't put my finger on the reason why. It was only after an occasion when I felt really stupid and conned that I recognized I'd been hooked into a mind game. He thought he was better than anyone else and looked down his nose at everyone. He asked me, in a whiny voice, a question about some paperwork. He was in the victim position and I, being eager to please, leaped into the rescuer position and told him the answer. But no sooner had I explained how the paperwork was to be done, he began to argue with me and went on and on, wanting me to admit that I might have gotten it wrong. He had switched positions to persecutor and I was then the victim. He phoned the supervisor for the answer, obviously disregarding what I'd told him, and when he was told the same answer as I'd given him, he said that my explanation hadn't been clear. I was so mad that I left the office to cool off, and that's when it hit me that I felt conned, and realized that I'd been hooked into a mind game. I already know that the reason for playing mind games is to generate drama so that people can 'stay connected' without dropping their guard and feeling vulnerable. But I wondered what his *motivation* could be. And then it dawned on me that he needed to see himself as superior to others and would deliberately go out of his way to make others look stupid so that he could maintain the perception he had of himself. Once I understood it, I was able to stay out of the game by avoiding the hooks."

"How?" Rocky asks.

"I became very sensitive to what he was saying, and I was on my guard. When I got back to my desk, he started again. He always wanted the last word. He kept asking me questions. I knew that he was going to argue with any answers I gave him, so I didn't take the bait. I kept saying, 'I don't know' over and over, and eventually he got tired and stopped."

"Man, that sounds like hard work," Marcus says.

"It was," Miss Tina replies, "but I was determined not to allow him to hook me into his games, just so he could end up feeling good and I'd end up feeling stupid."

Miss Tina glances at her watch and says, "Let's do one more example. Who can think of a time when you've been in one of these three positions but unexpectedly found yourself in another? Who's felt conned?"

Velvet puts her hand up. "I hated my mom because I felt used."

"How so?" Miss Tina asks.

"Because all the time she was falling apart, I was there for her. It was like I was her parent, not the other way around." She studies the diagram on the flipchart. "I guess I was in the rescuer position and she was the victim. Everything was going wrong for her. Then suddenly, when she found another man, she didn't want me around. She switched positions and ended up persecuting me—she put me in foster care—and I was the victim."

Miss Tina beams at her. "Oh Velvet, you're wonderful. You understand."

"Yeah, but I don't understand," she cries. "Why would she throw me away?"

"Oh, honey," Miss Tina says gently, "it's because she didn't know how to be truly intimate. She was desperate for Strokes, so she played mind games and chose a man who would play them with her. They operated on the drama triangle. If only she had believed that she had Warm Fuzzies in her fuzzy bag. If only she could have opened her heart and realized that she was a valuable human being who didn't need to settle for Cold Pricklies. All she had to do was to accept Warm Fuzzies into her life and then she'd never have chosen a man who played mind games, and there's no way that she could ever have given you away."

A tear rolls down Velvet's face.

Chapter Ten

I reach over and place my hand on Velvet's arm. I'm shocked to see her cry. She always seems so strong. I guess Miss Tina and Ken just struck a nerve. I know how she feels.

Ken speaks. "But it's not a mind game if two people communicate between two positions and don't switch to another."

We all look baffled.

"Okay," he says, turning towards Miss Tina. "If I'm in the rescuer position and Miss Tina's in the victim position, this is what it'll sound like if it's not a mind game."

Miss Tina jumps up and stands next to Ken.

Ken says, "I can't believe that they treated you that way. You poor thing. I'll speak to management if you wish."

Miss Tina says, "Oh, thank you for helping me. I feel so awful. They've treated me so badly."

Ken points to the diagram on the flipchart and says, "Okay, I'm in the rescuer position and Miss Tina's in the victim position, but that's because she truly is a victim and I'm truly trying to help her, to rescue her. This is *not* a mind game. Do you understand?" he asks.

We nod.

They go back to their seats and Miss Tina asks, "How are you feeling?"

Several of us say, "Horrible."

Alfie says, "I can't even begin to work out the mind games my mom and dad and his boyfriend were playing, but I know they *were* playing games because I felt conned and manipulated all the time. They treated me like a possession; they fought over me, yet I never felt that they wanted me. It felt as if they just wanted to deprive each other of me. Man, this is crap. I hate it."

Ken responds. "I know. It's tough. But now that you know about mind games you can stay out of them."

"How?" Alfie asks bitterly. "What can *I* do?"

Ken smiles at him and says, "Recognizing mind games is the first step to staying out of them. Refuse to play. Walk away. Be respectful, but determined. Say, 'This doesn't feel right to me,' and hold your head high. In your circumstances, if your parents try to put you in the middle to score points, ask them respectfully to leave you out of it. Be respectful, though. When you walk away from the drama triangle, you leave the mind game. The other person then doesn't have anyone to play with, and the fact that you've walked away invites them to interact in a more honest way."

Alfie sounds really angry. "I'm not going to let anyone mess with me again. I don't want to be dragged into this—it's not happening, right!"

"Me neither," Rocky agrees. "No way."

"I'm going to be on guard, watching for the switch in positions," Lexi says. "Man, this is clever stuff, but I'm going to be smarter. I am *not* going to let anyone hook me into playing stupid games. I'm tired of fricking Cold Pricklies, and Tepid Ticklies, and I won't put up with it anymore. I'm done."

"Me too," the kids say one by one. I join in.

"Another thing you can do is to try to communicate without stepping onto the drama triangle at all," Miss Tina says.

Some kids appear confused.

"Mind games can start through misunderstandings, so if you try to communicate honestly, mind games can be avoided. You can do this through a process called *active listening*. Ken and I will show you what we mean."

Ken stands. Miss Tina says, "Think back to when Maizy said that she was confused about sarcasm. She heard Lexi say one thing but interpreted it as another. It would have been simple for them to step onto the drama triangle. Remember how Lexi said, 'Maizy should give out Warm Fuzzies to her mom and sister; then perhaps things would get better between them.' Maizy felt irritated. She saw it as a Cold Pricklie, but Lexi was really trying to help her. Maizy misunderstood and could easily have stepped into the victim position, seeing Lexi in the persecutor position. If Maizy had reacted to the irritation she felt without expressing her feelings honestly, she would have switched to the position of persecutor and poor Lexi would have ended up in the position of victim—a mind game."

I glance at Lexi and smile at her.

Miss Tina continues and says, "Misunderstandings can be avoided by *active listening*. Active listening is about *really* listening and truly *hearing* what someone is saying to you. It's one of the most valuable lessons you'll ever learn, so listen up. Ken and I are going to show you how it's done."

Ken clears his throat.

"It's simple," Miss Tina says. "All you have to do is listen to what someone says to you and check it out with them. She quotes what Lexi says to me. "Ken, if you give out Warm Fuzzies to your mom and sister, perhaps things would get better between you all." She looks at Ken and says, "What did you *hear* me say?"

Ken puts his hands on his hips in defiance, mirroring my irritation, and says, "I heard you criticize me. I heard you picking on me."

My face burns.

Miss Tina turns towards us and says, "Because I've checked it out with him to make sure he understands what I'm saying, I can correct any misunderstanding between us. If I hadn't asked him what he *heard* me say, not *what* I said, we could have stepped onto the drama triangle or he could have walked away angry at me, and I wouldn't have understood why. I want to let him know that I've heard his confusion—I want to validate his feelings, so this is what I'm going to say."

She turns to Ken and says, "I'm sorry if your feelings are hurt, but that wasn't what I meant at all. I was just making a suggestion. I was trying to help you." She then says, "What did you *hear* me say, Ken?"

"I heard you being kind to me. You made it right. I felt angry and defensive, but I see that I misunderstood you. You were trying to help me. I'm sorry."

Miss Tina turns towards us, and says, "See how intimate we are being. Isn't it wonderful? There will always be misunderstandings between people because we're human and unsure of ourselves, but if we use *active listening* and check out what the other person *really* means, we can be intimate. That means we never have to swap Cold Pricklies or Tepid Ticklies again, and we'll never play mind games and step onto the drama triangle. How awesome is that?"

My heart swells and I sigh. Miss Tina tells us we've worked hard and lets us go.

We go swimming and the sea is warm and salty. I float on my back and kick my legs, letting the water fill my ears. Everything's muffled as I stare up into the endless blue sky. Seaweed floats around me, a watery ballet, in time to the rhythmic waves that lap over my body. I feel as if I'm in heaven where no one can hurt me.

I think of Mrs. White and her gift to me. The warmth of the sun on my body is nothing compared to the warmth in my heart for my sweet, elderly friend. I will never forget her, and I will never waste the gift she's given me. I'm going to go to college and make her proud of me. I take a resolute deep breath and get water up my nose. I stand up and wade through the water, coughing.

"Are you okay?" Marcus asks with concern on his face.

I laugh. "Yes, I'm fine. I was dreaming and forgot I was in the water."

Velvet hands me a tissue from her bag and I blow my nose. Lexi hands me a can of soda and I flop down on the sand, letting the warm sun dry the beads of water from my body.

"Group was something else today," Marion says. "I don't think I'll ever look at things the same way again."

"I know what you mean," I say over another

cough. I clear my throat and take a swig from the can. "I'm going to be on guard and really trust my feelings in the future. If I feel conned, I'm going to take a step back and think about the positions on the drama triangle and see if I've switched from one to another."

"Yeah, although it's deep," Lexi says, "it's pretty easy to do when you put it that way."

"I know. It's like Miss Tina and Ken have given us a tool," Velvet agrees. "We just have to check out our feelings, see if they suddenly change, and match them to the drama triangle. How awesome is that?"

"It's still going to take some practice, though," Marcus warns. "I mean, Miss Tina told us how hard it was when that guy kept badgering her with questions. She really had to work hard to avoid the hook before he eventually gave up."

I think of Lesley. "I think that if someone is used to hooking you into their mind games, they'll be surprised when you don't bite, and they'll try even harder to hook you in," I say. "I imagine my sister would be very hard to stop. I'm going to try, though," I add.

"But what confuses me," Lexi says, with a frown on her face, "is the *motivation* to play mind games. I understand that the reason is to generate drama so that you'd—what did Miss Tina call it—'stay connected to someone without dropping your guard or feeling vulnerable,' but what is a person's motivation to play mind games? That doesn't seem so obvious to me."

I think about my mom and dad. "My mom and dad's mind games were exactly the same as Miss Tina and Ken's role play. I wonder what their motivation was?"

We fall silent for a moment, searching for an answer that makes sense.

Velvet speaks first. "I think your mom sounds as if she likes to be in charge, and maybe your dad's scared of women." She grins at me and I can't help but laugh. She's just described my parents.

"Yeah, but *why*? Why would mom be so controlling, which she is," I add, "and why would Dad be afraid of getting close to a woman? I really think he is, because he's marrying another controlling woman. I mean, what's all that about?"

We fall silent again, thinking. A man driving an ice cream van stops by us and we walk over to buy one. I get a wafer cone with chocolate ice cream swirled in it and candy on the top. We sit in silence facing the sea, eating the ice cream, deep in thought.

"Maybe your dad's not very good with responsibility, and leaves it all to your mom," Alfie chips in after a while.

Marcus turns to me with strawberry ice cream on his top lip and says, "Y'know, something must have happened to your parents when they were kids to make them behave the way they do now. I mean, I'd hate to marry someone that would push me around and tell me what to do. Why would your dad do that, twice?"

I lick a creamy drip that rolls down the outside of my cone.

"Maybe he learned how to behave from his dad," Harriet suggests. "Could your dad's mom have been bossy and controlling and he learned how to behave around that type of woman from watching his dad?"

"But wouldn't he want a different life than his dad's?" Scott protests.

"Maybe it was all he knew," Velvet says wisely.

I finish my ice cream and wipe my mouth on the back of my hand. "But what I don't get is why would Mom be so mean to my dad—and he's really nice—if she thought that he might leave her if she pushed him too hard? It doesn't make any sense."

"It makes sense somehow," Velvet says. "We just have to figure out an answer that fits."

"I know. Maybe she was scared of men, and chose one that she could control so that she wouldn't feel so scared," Rocky chips in.

"Hey," Lexi says animatedly, "that would fit. If for some reason she was scared of men, then the motivation to play mind games would be that she'd feel safe. She'd successfully keep your dad at a distance by picking on him."

I look at her and suddenly I want to cry, because

her explanation really *does* fit. Mom's motivation to play mind games must be that she'd feel safe by pushing Dad away, but Dad's motivation—well, that's not so easy. I think of Velvet and Alfie's suggestions. Perhaps Dad *was* scared of women or maybe he just didn't like responsibility. I think he was scared of Lesley. He wouldn't stand up to her and as a father he should have. It's suddenly all too much for me to deal with, so I jump up and run towards the sea. I want the water in my ears again so that it deadens the sounds and the reality around me.

"Are you okay?" Marcus asks me at dinner. "You've been quiet since we talked about your parents."

I pop a fry into my mouth and talk around it. "Yeah, I'm okay." I dip another one into some ketchup, and say, "It was hard to hear everyone's thoughts about my parents' motivations to play mind games. I wanted to cry because it made me see how vulnerable they were, and that their arguments and mind games were just noise to hide what was really going on with them."

He nods knowingly.

"It makes me feel sad," I say quietly, as I draw patterns in the ketchup with a fry.

"I know. I've been trying to figure out the motivations for my parents' mind games. It's not easy. It feels like doing a thousand-piece jigsaw puzzle that's all in black. I want to hammer the pieces together and make them fit, but I know I have to search for the right piece," he says, balancing peas on his fork.

"I can't believe that I'm thinking this way," I say. "The things I've learned have totally changed my way of thinking. I can't believe the change in myself."

"I know," he replies. "That's how it is for me. Before I came to Beach Haven I was full of anger and hate. I loved my mom but I was so mad at her for having an affair. Dad went crazy and kicked her out. I love them both, but now I feel I have to choose between them all the time."

The fry in my hand turns cold as I listen to Marcus's story. He's always so quiet in group and never says much about his parents. My heart feels full of Warm Fuzzies for him, as he trusts me enough to show me his pain. I don't say anything, I just nod.

"I've tried to figure out my parents' motivations to play mind games, but it's hard," he says, glancing at his empty fork. The peas have slid off and some have rolled across the table. "My dad's a cop and there were times when he could be mean to Mom. I hate to say that because I feel like I'm being disloyal to him." He shakes his head and puts his fork down. There are obviously more important things on his mind than food. "But that's how I feel. I hated to hear my mom cry. It twisted my guts."

I drop my fry, my appetite gone, and look at him,

my heart hurting for him. He has tears in his eyes.

"Somewhere deep inside me, I think I understand why Mom had an affair. I think Dad drove her to it. I'd never say that to either of them, of course, but that's what I think."

I struggle for something to say and dig into all the things Miss Tina and Ken have taught us. "Did they share any Warm Fuzzies?" I ask lamely.

He wipes his nose on the back of his hand and struggles with himself. He shakes his head vehemently. "No, never. I can honestly say that I never saw them ever give each other a Warm Fuzzie. That's not to say that they didn't give them to me; they did. That's what makes it so confusing. How could they be nice to me and yet vile to each other? They didn't seem to realize how much that hurt me."

He turns to look out the window and I stay silent because I know he's trying to compose himself. I want to tell him that he doesn't have to—it's fine for him to cry in front of me—but something about the stiffness in his back and his clenched fists tells me to be quiet and let him work it out in his own way. My dinner's gotten cold and I don't want it anymore, so I push my plate away and take a gulp of my lemonade, waiting for him to reconnect with me.

He turns towards me, ignoring the tears in his eyes, and I feel that he's just given me a gift. He trusts me to see his pain. "What do *you* think my parents' motivation was to play mind games?"

I try to put myself in his shoes. "You said that your dad could be mean, so your mom was probably afraid, right?" I check with him, looking into his eyes for confirmation.

He nods and I carry on.

"Um, uh, it sounds like your dad doesn't really like women."

"I remember him talking about when I was born and he said, 'Thank God you were a boy.' I felt bad when he said it but I didn't understand why," he says.

"Maybe the motivation for his mind games was that he could confirm that women were no good." As I speak, it suddenly becomes clearer to me. "And when she had an affair, it proved what he'd always felt—he didn't like women."

My face is scrunched in a grimace, one that reflects my uncertainty as I think aloud.

"That makes sense," he says quietly. "I've been trying to figure out where they were on the drama triangle. Dad was definitely the persecutor and Mom the victim. I can't see that either of them rescued each other, but the switch would have been when Mom had an affair and hurt him. I guess, she finally had some power over him after years of him controlling her. Man..."

I prompt him to go on. "What d'you think your mom's motivation was to play mind games?"

"I think she was angry with my dad. Even when

he was nice to her, she had a silent attitude," he says, frowning.

"A silent attitude?" I ask.

"Yeah, it was like she was angry with him yet couldn't say it, so she was moody and would deliberately do things to piss him off," Marcus says. "She'd let him know how much she hated him without ever saying a word."

"What, like being passive aggressive?" I ask.

"Yes."

"So her motivation to play mind games was...?"

He frowns, trying to find the piece of the puzzle that fits. Suddenly his face lights up. "She used to tell me how mean her dad was to her. Perhaps her motivation to play mind games was to confirm that all men were bullies. Yes, that must be it. That fits."

He looks at my cold, congealed dinner, and asks, "Are you done?" I nod, and we take our trays to the kitchen. I follow him past the nice lady that cooks for us, out of the dining room and through the side door that leads to the playground.

We sit on the swings and sway with our legs. Marcus clears his throat. "Thanks for listening to me," he says.

"Oh, it's nothing." But I don't actually believe that. It's not nothing to listen to another person. In fact, it feels like sharing Warm Fuzzies to me.

The next week goes by in a heady determination to understand all the hooks to mind games that might come our way and to learn how to avoid them. It's not easy but we work hard to figure it all out. I really want to know how to stay out of the mind games Lesley plays, as I refuse to be a slave to her manipulation of me.

The day finally arrives for my next family session and I'm filled with dread. Before we go into the room, Miss Tina takes my hands and says, "What I want you to do is to tell everyone exactly what you feel and let's see what they all say and do. We're going to show them how they interact now and how different it would be if you'd all use *active listening* to communicate." She grins at me. "Don't worry, it'll be all right; we're going to teach them what you've learned here." She gives me a hug before opening the door.

Everyone's already seated when I walk into the room. I feel really nervous, wondering what's going to happen. The first thing I notice is Ronan isn't there. I don't know if I'm relieved or upset. Millie and Lesley are sitting together and I feel afraid. They nudge each other as Mom and Dad come over to give me a hug. Carol and Leo say, "Hi" but don't get up. Millie's other sisters and Timmy aren't there. I sit next to Miss Tina.

Miss Tina smiles at everyone and starts to talk. "Thanks for coming. What we hope to do today is to figure out how you can all live peacefully together, not as a broken family, but as a new blended family."

There's tension in the room. Carol looks angry, as if she's here against her will. I wish she wasn't here. I wish Millie and Lesley weren't here, either, but I wish Ronan was, and as I think of him, I swallow hard. Why isn't he here? I feel hurt, but then I feel angry with him. He must still believe Millie over me. Anger flares through me as I relive the injustice of Millie blaming me for blackening her eye and Ronan believing her. How could he?

I think about what Miss Tina's just told me to do—I've got to tell everyone exactly what I feel. I glance at her and she gives me a slight nod and I feel strength. I let my anger spill over. "I want to know why all of you would believe that I could blacken Millie's eye. I admit I slapped her when she was picking on me, but I didn't punch her."

"You did, too," Millie whines.

"Yes, you did," Lesley says,

"How would you know?" I raise my voice. "You weren't even there."

"Well, somebody blackened my daughter's eye," Carol says.

"It wasn't me," I say as calmly as I can.

"If it wasn't Maizy," Miss Tina says, "who was it?" She looks at Millie.

Millie gets very red but persists in blaming me. Her voice is shrill and loud as Lesley eggs her on.

Carol glares at me and says that I'm lucky she didn't call the police. My stomach's in shreds.

"Listen to yourselves," Miss Tina says quietly. Millie mutters under her breath. "I'm sorry. I may not have known Maizy very long, but I've watched her learn and grow. She takes responsibility for her behavior, and if she says she didn't punch Millie in the eye, I believe her. I just wonder why everyone in this room doesn't."

Dad is the first to speak. "I believe her." He turns to me and says, "I've never believed that you could hurt anyone. I'm sorry I didn't speak up for you. I should have, I know."

My heart swells with love for him. Finally, he stands up for me. Millie starts to protest, but Miss Tina holds up her hand and Millie closes her mouth, her words unsaid, but hate alive on her face. Lesley glances around the room, suddenly unsure of herself.

"Thanks, Dad," I say, my anger dissipating.

Miss Tina's voice is even and calm. She glances between Mom and Carol and changes the subject. "And how are you two getting along?"

I cringe, waiting for them to start shouting, but they seem taken off guard and don't say anything.

"How is it for you, Dad?" Miss Tina persists.

He speaks out without being shy, and he stands up for himself. Perhaps having Miss Tina here gives him courage. "It's really hard," he says. "I feel pulled and pushed from every direction. I'm trying to do the right thing for my girls and for Carol's kids, but I don't seem to be able to do anything right. Frankly, I'm tired of being the bad guy all the time."

I smile at him, feeling proud.

"Why do you say that?" Carol snaps. "You make it sound as if there's a problem. You're with *me* now. *She* just needs to leave you alone," she glares at Mom.

"What!" Mom shrieks.

Carol leans forward and there's hate on her face. "You're constantly calling him."

"You bitch," Mom cusses.

Leo speaks, and we all look at him. Usually he doesn't have anything to say. "If he didn't keep coming around to our house, perhaps we wouldn't be sitting here."

"What do you mean, 'he keeps coming around to your house'?" Carol looks at Leo and then at Dad. "What's he talking about?" she demands of Dad.

Dad seems to shrink. "I'm not *always* at their house. I check on them sometimes, okay?"

Carol looks outraged. "Are you cheating on me?" she asks Dad.

"Well, that's rich," Mom says sarcastically.

Dad looks at Carol uncomfortably. "Of course not," he says. "Look, I was married for eighteen years; I can't just turn my back on them." He sounds anguished. He glances at me and adds, "And I don't want to either. I miss you guys, all of you."

Carol looks like she's about to burst.

"I love you, Carol," Dad says. "I'd never have left my family if I didn't, but I have to make sure they're okay."

"Yeah, but you don't need to," Leo says. "I'm there now. You're in the way."

"Hey, hang on a minute," Mom turns on him. "Don't say that. You don't have any right."

"I don't have any right?" Leo sounds affronted. "I thought we were together."

"We are, but don't tell me who can come into the house and who can't," Mom snaps.

"Well, excuse me," Leo bites back. He pushes his chair away as he stands up. "I guess if I have no rights, I don't need to be here." We all look at him as he stomps out of the room.

"Hey, wait for me," Millie calls out. "I don't need to be here either. Nobody believes anything I say, so I'm not staying." She cusses as she leaves the room.

Lesley glances at me and smirks. She turns to Mom and says, "I don't know why you brought me back here, either," as she gets up and follows Millie.

I look at Miss Tina and she smiles serenely at me, totally unruffled by the undignified mess that's exploded in the room.

Chapter Eleven

Miss Tina takes charge. "This is most disappointing," she says to Mom, Dad and Carol. "I guess we now know who is committed to making this new family work, and who isn't."

I feel relieved when she puts it like that, because Lesley, Millie and Leo have just shown us that they don't really care about our family.

Miss Tina says, "What you've all just witnessed is the noise that stops everyone from *really* listening to each other, so let's really express our feelings and *truly* hear what each other is saying." Miss Tina turns to Carol and says, "It's only natural that your fiancé is going to worry about his first family. He's a good man. Would you really want to be with someone who could so easily turn his back on his family? I mean, if he *could*, would you feel secure with him?"

Carol opens her mouth to say something but

shuts it as Miss Tina's question hits home.

"I was very impressed with you two last week," Miss Tina glances between Mom and Dad. "Carol, if you weren't feeling so afraid at the moment..."

Carol butts in. "What do you mean, afraid? I'm not afraid."

Miss Tina persists. "There's nothing wrong in feeling afraid."

"I'm not afraid," Carol raises her voice.

Miss Tina remains calm. "I believe you are, my dear, and it's perfectly normal when you're with someone who's left their partner for you. How can you be sure that he won't do the same to you?"

Carol glances at Dad, who looks really uncomfortable. Mom sits stiffly in her chair.

"As I was saying," Miss Tina continues, "I wish you'd been here last week and heard their honesty. I was really impressed. Both looked at their behavior and both vowed to change, and both recognized that their marriage was over and had been for some time."

Carol has tears in her eyes.

Miss Tina asks, "What did you just hear me say, Carol?"

"What?"

Miss Tina is patient and repeats her question, "What did you hear me say?"

"Um, I heard you praising them for wanting to change," Carol mumbles miserably. "That makes me feel like it's me with the problem."

Miss Tina helps her out. "I'm going to teach you a process called *active listening* so that you can avoid misunderstandings in the future. Active listening is about *really* listening and truly *hearing* what someone is saying to you. It's simple. All you have to do is listen to what someone says to you and check it out with them, and not allow yourself to be pulled away from the point."

Mom, Dad and Carol listen and don't say a word.

Miss Tina explains. "Carol, you didn't listen to everything I'd said, but honed in on one bit only and interpreted what I'd said as if I was picking on you. Active listening, checking out and listening to what someone is saying, will help you to avoid misunderstandings, and will also enable you to become closer. If you don't check out what each other's saying, you can get caught up in the noise you just heard before the others left." She grins and says, "And no one hears anything when there's that much noise going on."

Dad smiles bleakly at Miss Tina.

There's a flipchart in the corner of the room and Miss Tina goes over to it with a pen in her hand. "We're going to use this formula to help you practice active listening." She writes,

What did you hear me say?

I heard you say xxx.

Explain.

What did you hear me say now?

Miss Tina returns to her chair.

"Okay, Carol, let's use this formula to help you communicate better. 'What did you hear me say'?"

Carols glances at the flipchart and parrots, "I heard you say, um, that it was *my* fault that everything's going wrong."

Miss Tina smiles at Carol. "Good job, dear. Now, the next part of the formula is where I explain what I really meant, and you have to listen to all of it, okay?" Carol nods.

Miss Tina begins to explain what she really meant so that there can be no misunderstanding in Carol's mind. "I said that I wish you'd been here last week and heard their honesty, and that I was really impressed because both looked at their behavior and both vowed to change. They recognized that their marriage was over and had been for some time. I said it in order to try to make you feel more secure. If you'd been a fly on the wall, you'd have seen that your fiancé loves you very much and you have no need to feel afraid that he'll go back to his ex-wife."

Carol is close to tears.

Miss Tina then says, "What did you hear me say now?"

A tear rolls down Carol's face as she answers. "I heard you tell me my fiancé loves me very much and

I don't have to be afraid that he'll go back to his ex-wife."

Dad takes her hand and smiles at her.

"Awesome!" Miss Tina cries. "Think back to when you were all talking at once, shouting, throwing accusations at each other. No one was listening; it was just noise. If you can use this formula to express your feelings honestly, then you have no need to shout or be angry. Just say how you feel respectfully, and ask the other person if they heard you right."

I speak up. "Yes, but if I try the formula with Lesley, she'll only hear what she wants to hear. She's not interested in trying to understand my feelings."

Miss Tina smiles sadly. "My sweet child, you can only change yourself, no one else, remember?"

Carol speaks quietly. "I find it difficult because I can tell that you," she glances at Dad, "still love her."

"Of course I do," Dad says softly, but with strength. "She's the mother of my children, but I don't love her the same way I love you. You have nothing to fear."

Miss Tina says gently, "Don't you see that if you cling to him too tightly out of fear, if you try to control him, you'll push him away."

Miss Tina hands Carol a box of tissues and says, "It's very sad when a relationship that starts out in good faith ends, and it's only natural to grieve for the loss. It's like a death. But just because people grieve after a divorce, it doesn't mean that they want each other back. You have nothing to fear, Carol."

Something weird and amazing is happening in this room. Mom's vicious tongue is silenced, Dad seems taller and resolute, and Carol appears softer. She faces Mom, mascara smudged beneath her eyes. "I'm *so* sorry. We didn't set out to hurt you. I tried to fight my feelings for a long time," she says, falteringly.

Mom looks up and meets her eyes.

Dad speaks out, "So did I."

"It just happened. I'm *so* ashamed of what happened on New Year's Eve. I was nervous about the party and I'd been drinking. It was totally wrong and I hate that you felt so humiliated. And you're right, I behaved like a whore."

Mom shakes her head, as if she's embarrassed by the word. "No, I'm sorry, I shouldn't have called you that. I was crazy, that's all. I didn't know what to do. It was such a shock. I lost it, I guess."

They embark on a strange dance of apology that excludes everyone else in the room. I say nothing.

"I know you were angry," Carol says, "and you had every right to be, but it seems that the angrier you got, the more defensive I became. Every time he called you, or went over to your house, I couldn't stand it. I felt that you were trying to take him back—to do to me what I'd done to you." She starts crying again. "It hurts so bad. I don't know how you endured it. I'm *so* sorry."

Mom has tears in her eyes now. I can't believe it. Something like peace settles over us and my heart soars. Dad smiles at me and Miss Tina beams.

"I'm so proud of you all," Miss Tina says. "You are really listening to each other. You've said some painful things, but said them respectfully. I have such high hopes for you all, that you are going to be able to build a wonderful blended family where everyone has a special, valued place—where everyone is respected."

Mom and Carol dab their eyes and Dad clears his throat.

"What you have to realize is that, while you've been jostling for position and fighting, your kids have joined in. Some of them have been persecutors, rescuers, and victims, but all have been seeking to find a place in this new blended family. If you can find resolution and present a united front, your kids will settle down and stop all their drama," Miss Tina continues.

I understand exactly what she's saying—persecutor, rescuer and victim—the drama triangle. Lesley and Millie are the persecutors, Ronan is a rescuer and I'm the victim. I feel sick with the realization of it all. Silence hangs in the air as we each take in what Miss Tina's said.

"What's done is done; let's move forward," she says. "Stand firm together so that your children don't have to fight to get your attention anymore. Let each child know that they have a valued place in this new blended family you're trying to build. If you can't do this, you condemn yourselves and your children to a life of drama and animosity. You all deserve better."

Carol takes a deep breath and nods, filling herself with resolve.

"I'm going to try," she looks at Mom and adds, "if you will, too. Can you forgive me for hurting you?"

"I can't say it'll be easy, but I'm going to try, too," Mom says. "I know I drove my husband away. Part of it is my fault."

"And part of it is my fault, too," Dad says.

Miss Tina turns to me and says, "Maizy, you've been very quiet. What are you thinking?"

I shake my head. "I can't believe you're all talking it out. You sound like me and the kids in group."

Miss Tina laughs and faces the adults. "And *that* my friends is a compliment indeed."

I grin. Yes, I guess it is.

Dad turns to Miss Tina and is suddenly serious. "What can we do to stop the kids from fighting? It's gotten so bad that I don't know what to do."

Mom and Carol face Miss Tina, too.

"All the time they're jostling for position, they'll try to hook you in by forcing you to take sides. Stay out of any arguments. Say, 'I'm sure you can work it out; after all, you're family now.' Dad and Carol, be loving to each other in front of all the children without being overtly sexual; no kid can stand the idea of their parents having sex, let alone having to witness foreplay!"

I shudder.

"Mom and Carol, be respectful to each other and cheerful on the phone," Miss Tina continues, "so that when the kids see that you aren't fighting, they'll have nothing to fight against." She grins. "They'll probably be confused at first and try to hook you all into the drama they've become used to, but you'll be one step ahead of them now. Gradually, when they see that you are a united front, with their best interests at heart, they'll give up and accept that you are one big, beautiful, blended family."

Mom exhales, turns to Miss Tina and says, "I've got something to say."

"Go ahead."

"On New Year's Eve I was so upset that I did something bad. Leo had been badgering me for a date for months and I'd always told him to get lost, but that night I was so hurt that I wanted to do *anything* to hurt you," she looks at Dad.

Mom looks at Miss Tina for support. "I didn't even

like him. I certainly didn't *want* him." I cringe as memories of the grunting and groaning from Mom's bedroom flood my mind. "Sorry, Maizy," she winces, when she sees the look on my face.

Her jaw is set and her breathing slows. She grabs the sides of her armchair and says resolutely, "I don't want him in my life. I'm going to kick him out. I want to make this right." Something shifts on her face that speaks of pain. "I want..." she whispers, "I want what you two have." Dad and Carol glance at each other tenderly, and Mom continues, "I don't want to be with someone for the wrong reasons."

Miss Tina smiles at Mom. Dad and Carol hold hands and I look from one to the other, amazed that things could turn out so well. I can't believe that Mom and Carol are going to be friends, that Lesley and Millie won't be able to get me into trouble, and Leo is going to be thrown out of our house. This is amazing.

Suddenly I have something to say. "Carol, I want to promise on my honor that I did not blacken Millie's eye."

Miss Tina looks at Carol and she asks, "What did you hear Maizy say?"

"I heard her trying to make me believe that she didn't hurt my daughter," Carol says.

"Use the formula," Miss Tina tells me. "Explain yourself respectfully, Maizy."

"I didn't say that I didn't hurt Millie. I did. I

slapped her because I lost control of myself when she was picking on me. I'm really sorry, and I'm ashamed of myself for not walking away, but she baited me every single day. What I said was that I didn't blacken her eye."

Miss Tina smiles at me and I know she approves of my explanation of my behavior and feelings. She looks at Carol and says, "Carol, what did you hear Maizy say now?"

Carol clears her throat and takes a deep breath. "I think I hear you being very honest and responsible, and I believe you. If I'm honest with myself, I know Millie very well and I wouldn't put it past her to blacken her own eye, or get a friend to do it, just to get someone else into trouble. She gets Molly and Mandy into trouble all the time."

Miss Tina beams at Carol. "I'm so proud of you," she says.

Just then the door bursts open. Lesley and Millie stand united together, demanding to go home.

"This isn't fair," Lesley bleats. "I've got to get ready for tonight. Mark's picking me up. C'mon! Let's go home. This is a waste of time."

Millie looks affronted. "I thought you were coming over tonight."

"Yeah, well, plans change," Lesley says callously. "Get over it."

"What?"

"Don't argue, girls, I'm sure you can work it

out. After all, you're family now," Dad says, trying to keep the amusement out of his voice. Mom and Carol turn away, trying not to smile.

Lesley and Millie are speechless when Carol hugs me and I let her. I call out, "Goodbye," as they all leave the room, and Lesley and Millie frown at each other as they follow Mom and Carol, who chat about their house plants. I want to laugh but I stifle it.

"I can't believe it," I say to Miss Tina.

"I can," she says. "It all comes down to active listening. It's all going to be all right, Maizy. Your three parents are going to be amazing." She hugs me.

I find the others on the beach and they ask me how my family session went. I feel really lighthearted and I'm amazed. "If someone had told me that my mom and Carol could be in the same room as each other without fighting, I'd never have believed them. It's like a miracle. *And* my dad stuck up for me and also for Mom. He was awesome." My eyes water, and I laugh as a tear rolls down my cheek. "I just can't believe it."

"How were Lesley and Millie?" Lexi asks.

"Awful," I say, "but they looked as if they'd been slapped when they saw Carol hug me. I don't know, they seemed to lose some of their steam. For once, I didn't feel afraid."

"It'll make a difference if your dad sticks up for you," Marcus says wisely.

He's right. It will. I love my dad so much. My heart is brimming with love for him, and as warmth breaks out on my face as a smile, I think of my mom. She was amazing today. She was as honest as the kids around me. She owned up to her behavior, faced her pain, and was determined to make things right, even though it was hard. Another tear rolls down my face.

"What?" Marcus asks. "What did I say?"

I shake my head, laughing through my tears. "I miss my mom."

Ken comes over to us and asks the guys if they'd like to help build go-carts in the garage beyond the playground. Lexi chooses to go with them, but we girls take a walk along the shore searching for shells and stones that have been shaped by the ocean's rhythmic waves. I have a handful by the time we head in for dinner. Velvet tells me that Miss Cassie has a little machine that washes and polishes the stones so that we can make them into necklaces or bracelets. I'm excited because I want to make something that will remind me of Beach Haven for the rest of my life.

The guys eat dinner with us, and even though they've washed their hands, they have black grease under their nails. They virtually ignore us and jabber away about ball bearings and axles. Marion rolls her eyes and says loudly, "As I was saying, I found an amazing stone today that I'm going to make into a necklace for my mom's birthday." The guys glance momentarily at her and look away without really registering what she's said, or her point. I grin at her and we burst out laughing. Guys!

Miss Cassie helps us to transform the rough stones into art and tells us that she's doing the same to us. She says that she is *processing* the stones, and when we've been through the "Beach Haven process" we'll be like polished gems. She's sweet. I like the idea of being a polished gem.

The next morning after breakfast we file into the Group Room. I'm eager to get back to Miss Cassie's classroom, but I know the main reason I'm here is not to polish stones and make necklaces, but to be in group, so I sit up in my chair and wait for Miss Tina to talk.

She turns to me and says, "Maizy, weren't your three parents awesome in your family session yesterday?"

I wince slightly when she says my *three* parents, but then the idea starts to sit well with me.

"Guys, you should have seen them learn and practice active listening. They started out in the drama triangle, shouting and yelling at each other, with no one really listening. Am I right, Maizy?"

I grin and say, "Not half. It was a mess."

"But once they stopped shouting and really listened to each other, and checked out what they really meant, everything changed. They walked away from the drama triangle and learned how to be close. It was awesome," Miss Tina tells enthusiastically.

She bends over to pick up a wad of papers under her chair and turns to us with a grin on her face.

"Now, you know how I love little stories. Well, here's one about people who are stuck in the drama triangle, who have to get the last word, and who refuse to listen. It's called, 'The Frightful Noise.'"

I settle back into my chair, feeling cozy and proud of my three parents.

Far, far way in the land that bobs in and out of view depending upon the sea mist, there was a great noise that deafened all the creatures who lived in the forests and on the mountains and those who roamed the plains. The Gods of the Trees could barely hear themselves think as they sat among their branches watching the people who lived beneath them.

At night when the noise subsided, the gods were able to hear each other and commented that it hadn't always been that way. They remembered the days when the only sounds that floated up to them in their sacred trees were the sounds of children laughing and playing and animals calling to each other. Birdsong wafted on the wind and even the delicate beating of butterfly wings could be heard by the gods. Children played, and when their parents called them, they came without arguing. They hugged each other and the children listened eagerly to their parents' stories, tales of merriment and wisdom, and the gods had marvelled at their creations in the land that bobbed in and out of view depending upon the sea mist.

Then one day the people beneath the great trees began to change. The gods didn't notice at first. They didn't notice that an entity called Ramad crept silently among the people who lived beneath them. The gods didn't realize that Ramad feared and loathed the closeness that kept the children and their parents connected to each other, and to the gods living above them. Ramad was like a subtle creeping disease, one that infected everyone silently, yet in that silence, a noise began to fill the air, a rumble at first, but one that became a roar that deafened everyone.

As the years went by Ramad lodged in the hearts of all those who lived beneath the trees, whispering hateful, mean things in the people's ears and instilling fear in their hearts. The people no longer believed that others cared about them, or that they could say what they thought and know that it would be honored and accepted. They had doubt in their hearts and they became defensive, feeling the need to defend themselves against others who were equally afraid of them.

Over the years the people became so afraid of

each other that they devised ways to avoid becoming too close to one another. Ramad glowed with pleasure, having succeeded in its mission, for it fed on fear, chaos and drama. It grew and strengthened among the people, as it whispered to them in their dreams, filling them with fear lest others get too close. The people, primed and defensive, bit harshly at those who dared to venture near, and when they spoke, they shouted, their fists clenched, ready to push others away for fear of them getting too close. No matter what anyone said, each argued, and as they became determined to have the last word, the noise grew louder and louder and no one could hear anything.

The Gods of the Trees watched helplessly, unable to hear themselves think over the din, and they watched their people, who had once been so close and connected to each other, divide and separate. It was an insidious split, one that the gods couldn't fathom. Although the people still lived beneath the trees, they separated into three distinct tribes called the Angst, the Villing and the Hurtz, and they fought, yet their fight was not that of fists but of words. The gods, far above, alert in their trees, winced as each person wounded the other, and they didn't know what to do to stop the noise that ravished the land. There was no reason for them to fight, yet the people were consumed with animosity. The noise grew so loud that the gods stuffed their fingers into their ears to block it out, and there was never a day when the Gods of the Trees did not despair over the tribes living beneath their sacred trees.

Daily life for each tribe member was hard, harsh and unbearable. The Angst were filled with hate and persecuted everyone they came across. They felt as if it was their right to tell others what they were doing wrong, and they grew in their righteousness and criticism every minute. The Villing tried to please everyone and felt helpless when they pleased no one. They tried so hard, yet when their efforts were ignored, they shouted their outrage and demanded the last word.

The third tribe, the Hurtz, after trying to get the last word, shrunk away from the Angst and the Villings. They didn't want anything to do with any of them, and they justified their actions to their children by recounting the monstrosities the two other tribes had inflicted upon them. They locked themselves in their homes alone with their bitterness, and when their pain became too great, they exploded in anger, shouting and blaming the other tribes.

The Gods of the Trees cried out to each other when they saw that their people were estranged and hated each other, and all the time Ramad laughed at the mischief it had caused. The noise was deafening as every man, woman and child was intent on having the last word, each failing to listen to the other, and each one fearful of being close to another human being. Yet they felt disquiet in their hearts, for deep within each person was the need to feel connected to other people. They were afraid.

And so this unhappy situation would have gone on forever if it hadn't been for a mother and her son who were traveling on a long journey to visit relatives at the end of the land. They arrived in the midst of the Angst, the Villing and the Hurtz one evening, tired from their journey. They sought an inn, a place to rest, and while the child's mother napped, the boy went in search of friends to play with.

He was unprepared for the noise that resounded through the trees, and he felt uncomfortable when children from each tribe tried to snare him into their midst, all the time berated the children from the other tribes. He'd never known such anger or the fear that flickered behind each child's eyes, and it made him afraid. He ran back to the inn to his mother, and she awoke, alarmed at the confusion on her son's face.

"There is something wrong with the people in this village," he cried, and his mother trusted him, for they were close and knew honesty.

"Do you know what it is?" his mother asked.

"No. It's nothing I've ever experienced before,

and I don't like it," he said. "I want to be friends with all the children, but they are nice to me yet mean to each other. I don't understand," he said with confusion on his face.

Each day the boy persevered, trying to get close to all the children in the Angst, the Villing and the Hurtz tribes, and although they each welcomed him, they loathed the other children who did not belong to their own tribe, and each night he went back to the inn, confused.

The Gods of the Trees watched him with hope in their hearts, for he was different from all the children in the divided village.

One day the boy stood amidst the children in the village who shouted as loud as their parents in order to have the last word, and he said very quietly, in almost a whisper, "I cannot hear you. I want to know what you're saying, all of you."

The children of the Angst, Villing and the Hurtz fell silent at once, straining to hear what he was saying.

"I want to know all of you," he repeated, and the children glanced at each other with confusion on their faces.

The little boy smiled at them all and whispered, "Let's get away from all the noise and play. C'mon, let's make a camp."

Excitement was alive on his face and all the children followed him, even though they felt uncertain and didn't know what to do as they left the noise behind them. Throughout the day he showed them how to work together to build a tree house, and they swung from ropes hanging over the branches and whooped with joy. The Gods of the Trees held their breath as the children played in their midst, none of them shouting, and none seeking to get the last word.

As the sunlight slipped behind the trees a small child said quietly, "I don't want to go home. This has been the best day of my life."

"It doesn't have to end," the boy said, "we can meet here again tomorrow."

And so they met every day and played together, sat and talked together and, since none felt the need to defend themselves from each other anymore, none felt the need to have the last word. They truly listened to each other and knew the closeness the Gods of the Trees had intended for their people.

Each evening the children returned to the village with heavy hearts, knowing that they had to join their tribes and listen to their parents berate the other tribes and their children. The parents were shouting so loudly, that when the children tried to tell them about their new friends, they could not hear, and didn't want to listen, for Ramad was still alive in their hearts.

The day came when the boy and his mother

had to continue their journey, and the children of the village wept as they left. Most of the parents continued to shout and berate their neighbors, but one or two parents were shocked into silence by the sight of their children's tears. They asked them why they were crying, yet they couldn't hear because the noise was too great, so the children led them to their camp away from the village. There among the sacred trees, with the gods listening and holding their breath, the children spoke and their parents listened for the first time in their lives. One child broke down and said that she couldn't stand the noise and animosity any longer and wanted to follow their new friend and his mother out of the village.

The parents looked at each other, aware that those who had to have the last word would never stop making the noise, so they took a deep breath and made a decision. They packed up their possessions that night and left the village during the temporary silence as their neighbors slept. They knew that those who were too afraid to allow themselves to become close to another human being would continue to fight and argue, relishing the drama that Ramad had instilled in their hearts, but they also knew that they couldn't live that way any longer.

They journeyed through the night, up over a mountain and down into a fertile valley, and by the time the sun began to glimmer on the horizon, they *rested and made it their home.*

The children and parents who had escaped the Angst, the Villing and the Hurtz lived in harmony from that day forth as the Gods of the Trees had intended. No one shouted or needed to get the last word, for everyone spoke gently to each other, and they listened and truly heard one another, as the boy had shown them.

Occasionally, when the wind was high, the noise from the Angst, the Villing and the Hurtz could be heard from afar, along with the groaning from the Gods of the Trees, and it was on those occasions that every man, woman and child who had left the chaos, drama and animosity in the village, with bravery in their hearts, rejoiced at the closeness they'd found by listening to each other.

Chapter Twelve

"**C**an I have a copy of that story for my parents?" I ask. My heart feels full as I realize that my parents and I have been brave enough to leave our "village" and to walk away from the noise, the drama triangle. We've left Lesley, Millie and Leo behind. I know I now live in a fertile valley, and I feel relieved. Suddenly I long to talk to Aunt Hettie and tell her everything that I've learned here at Beach Haven.

It dawns on me that because my family sessions have focused around Mom, Dad, Carol and Leo, Aunt Hettie has been pushed to the back of my mind. I call her later and it's wonderful to hear her voice.

"You sound so different," she cries. "Oh honey, I miss you. Your mom says you're coming home in a couple of days. I can't believe how different she sounds too."

"I'm coming home?" I ask, shocked. I feel as if she's just knocked the wind out of me.

"Your mom said you were doing so well that you're ready to come home," Aunt Hettie says. "Oh, sweetheart, didn't you know?"

"No, no one said." I have goose bumps on my arms. I don't want to go home. I want to stay at Beach Haven forever. I feel safe here. I don't want to talk anymore and tell Aunt Hettie I've got to go. She sounds disappointed, but my head's spinning and I can't make small talk.

I seek out Miss Tina and, as soon as I see her, I burst into tears. She puts her arm around me and asks what's the matter.

"My aunt says you're sending me home," I wail.

"Oh," she says seriously, and I can tell by her tone that it's true.

"Why didn't you tell me?"

"Oh my beautiful girl, I've just gotten off the phone with your mom and she must have called your aunt immediately. I was just coming to find you to talk it over," she says gently.

She takes me to her office and tells me to sit down. "I'm so impressed with your progress," she explains, "and your parents' progress, that there isn't much more we can do for you here. You all have the tools you need to be able to work everything out at home. I'm so proud of you all."

I don't want to hear her say she's proud of me.

I don't want to leave Beach Haven and my new friends. "It's not fair. The other kids don't have to go so soon. Why do I have to?" I demand.

"Everyone's situation is different," Miss Tina explains kindly. "Some of the others don't have a home to go to. Some have parents who refuse to come to family sessions and aren't interested in making things better in their families. We can't send those kids home to that environment, but you have loving parents. You have a home to go to and parents who care. It's time for you to go home and practice everything we've taught you here."

Tears pour down my face at the thought of leaving everyone I've come to love.

She takes my hand and pats it while I cry. "Sweetheart, we'll always be here. Beach Haven is a family; you may leave home but we'll always be here for you. We're on the end of a phone and you can always come to visit. It's not the end, it's the beginning."

My tears finally subside and she hands me a box of tissues. A stray thought pops into my head; there are always boxes of tissues around, boxes in every room. I blow my nose and wipe my face.

"When do I have to go?" I ask, dreading the answer.

"How about tomorrow? Then you can hang out tonight with the others and say your goodbyes in the way you want to." she suggests.

I nod miserably.

I see the others goofing around on the beach. Seagulls screech above me and the sun beats down on the powdery sand. I stand on the grassy ridge for a moment to take in the scene, wanting to imprint it indelibly onto my mind so that I will never forget this beautiful place. Velvet sees me standing there and calls to me. I tramp over the loose sand to where they're sitting.

"What's wrong?" Marcus asks the moment I sit down. He amazes me. He is like a finely tuned instrument, tuned in to anything that's out of sync. I'm certainly out of sync at the moment. I'm so mad at myself when I burst into tears and tell them that I'm due to leave tomorrow.

One by one they offer me comfort. I can call. I can visit. We'll stay in touch. We talk about what we've learned and how that makes us close like the kids who fled the land of noise. I smile through my tears when they use Miss Tina's story to make their point. Yes, I guess we all belong to that fertile valley, and even though I won't be with them in person each day, I'll be with them in spirit like the little boy who left on his journey with his mother.

I finish my necklace of stones from the beach during the afternoon, and although they are only pebbles washed up on the shore, to me they're precious gems, and I'll treasure it for the rest of my life.

We don't have any groups today as Miss Tina wants me to be free to be with the kids. I tell them tearfully what they mean to me and everyone hugs me. I spend the entire day crying, although much of the time I'm laughing too, as these kids are so goofy. In between messing around, they make suggestions about how to handle Lesley and Millie and I listen intently, taking in everything they say. I feel like a sponge, soaking up every drop of advice. I trust them and I'll use every tactic they suggest.

I don't eat very much at dinner; I'm not hungry, in fact I feel rather sick. I just sit there with the pizza on my plate going cold, listening to the others chatter. When they finish they leave to go to the living room to watch a movie. Marcus stays with me and I notice that he hasn't eaten his food either. We take our trays to the kitchen and apologize to the cook who asks if the food was all right. My eyes fill with tears again as she gives me a Warm Fuzzie. I tell her I'm leaving and she gives me a big hug, which makes me cry even more.

We leave the dining room, and we can hear the kids arguing about what movie to watch. Marcus asks me if I want to go outside. I nod and follow him out of the door, through the playground and over the grassy ridge. He sits on the sand and I sit beside him.

He's silent for a few minutes and then says, still staring at the sea, "I'm going to miss you, Maizy.

You've been a great friend to me. You've listened when I've rambled on. You've helped me figure stuff out. Thanks." He turns towards me. "I've learned a lot from you. You've never judged me. You've never given me any Cold Pricklies or Tepid Ticklies. I don't think I've ever felt closer to anyone in my whole life. You're my best friend."

I swallow hard. My head is swimming. Is he saying that he wants me to be his girlfriend? I hope not because I'm still not over Ronan.

"I feel closer to you than to my girlfriend at home," Marcus says, clearing up my thoughts instantly.

I turn towards him and smile. "Y'know, I think you're my best friend too," I say, meaning every word. Miss Tina and Ken have taught us about closeness, intimacy—intimacy without sex—I smile as I think of us all chanting in group, and I know exactly what they mean about intimacy. I've shared my deepest thoughts with Marcus and he's shared his with me. That's amazing.

He takes my hand and I grip his tightly, hoping that we'll be friends forever. He smiles at me. My tears have evaporated. I feel calm and peaceful. Suddenly I have no need to grieve about leaving Beach Haven. I'm taking something wonderful with me.

We sit there for what seems like ages until the sun slips past the horizon and darkness takes its place.

The seagulls finally quiet down and a warm breeze blows off the receding tide. The stars reclaim the sky and twinkle knowingly. Marcus lies back on the sand and tugs at me to lie down too. I do. I don't care if I get sand in my hair.

"Look," he whispers. "Look at the stars. Make a wish on one."

I look up into the heavens, an inky black patchwork with patterns waiting to be discovered. I see the North star shining brightly.

I grip Marcus's hand as I think of a wish. "I wish that I..." I struggle with the wish to stay at Beach Haven forever, but I know that's not possible and not right. "I wish that I can feel as close to other people as I do to you right now." I feel him squeeze my hand.

"Me too," he says.

We lie there without saying anything for some time, lost in the twinkling tapestry above us, our wishes a prayer.

A bell rings and we get up, knowing that it's time to be inside. I have sand all over me, in my hair and on my clothes, but I don't care. I feel wonderful inside for I've said goodbye in the way I wanted to, quietly and with meaning.

The next morning I shower and start to pack my things. I'm okay. I thought I'd be a basket case, howling and sobbing, but somehow last night with Marcus showed me what true closeness is, and nothing can take it away, not time or distance. I feel a sense of resolve. I'm going home and I'm going to use every tool Miss Tina, Miss Cassie and Ken have taught me. I'm going to make sure that I've only got Warm Fuzzies in my fuzzy bag, my heart, and I'm going to remind myself that I can only change myself and no one else. I will ask myself the question, "What did I do?" to force me to accept responsibility for my own behavior, but beyond that I'll walk away when I feel that someone is trying to hook me into playing mind games and entering the drama triangle. As I zip up my bag, I take a deep breath. I can do this.

Though I can't eat breakfast, I join everyone down in the dining room, and when Miss Tina walks into the room accompanied by Aunt Hettie, my stomach does a double flip. The time is coming when I have to say goodbye to everyone here, everyone I love, the honesty in this place and the unconditional support.

Aunt Hettie says hello to all the kids. The cook gives her a plate of breakfast and she sits with us. She seems fascinated by us, and the kids obviously like her because they answer all her questions, and then some.

"Well, I wish there had been places like Beach Haven when I was a kid," Aunt Hettie says. "I'd have signed up at the age of four."

Everyone laughs and I want to hug my aunt, but

she's so busy bantering with the kids that the moment passes. I determine that I'll hug her later for being such an awesome aunt.

Eventually the time comes, and after hugging everyone, Aunt Hettie and Miss Tina escort me to the front door.

My leaving Beach Haven occurs in a heady blur, one I choose to forget. My first real memory is of Aunt Hettie pulling into our drive and Mom bursting through the front door. I get out of the car, my heart heavy, although I know it's going to be okay. I look over towards Mrs. White's house. There's a "for sale" sign planted in the garden with a smaller sign with the word "SOLD" plastered over it. I feel offended. I don't want Mrs. White's house to be sold. I don't want other people to be in her house, yet I accept it because I know things change.

Mom hugs me so hard that I feel she may crush me. Something has changed in her. Her face is serene, although excited.

"I couldn't wait for you to come home," she gushes all over me. She pulls me by the arm into the living room and we sit on the sofa. Aunt Hettie follows.

"I did it, baby. I told Leo to go," Mom says excitedly. "He's gone. I feel so relieved. Dad's been over and he brought Carol, and I can't believe it, but it was okay. I thought it would be awkward, but it wasn't. Can you believe that?" she gushes.

I glance at Aunt Hettie who smiles and nods re-assuringly, saying, "I was here. It was amazing. I wouldn't have believed it if I hadn't seen it with my own eyes."

"Dad read the riot act to Lesley and told her exactly what she could do and what she couldn't, and we stood there, the three of us, backing each other up, and..." Mom giggles like a girl, "...she was so shocked that she didn't say a word."

"You're kidding," I gasp, feeling a grin slip onto my face at the thought.

"Yes, I couldn't believe it, either. She just went to her room and has been in a sulk ever since, but at least she hasn't been shouting. It's a start," Mom adds.

"I hope she doesn't go back to being her usual self now that I'm home," I say, worried. Although I have all the tools Beach Haven has given me, I still don't look forward to coping with Lesley.

"Well, if she tries to, we'll just have to deal with it. Not you, baby, I, your dad and Carol. Lesley is not going to run anything anymore," Mom says adamantly.

I can't believe my mom. She sounds so differ-ent and I feel overwhelming love for her. "Can I give you a Warm Fuzzie?" I ask, with a twinkle in my eye.

"Oh please," she cries, and we hug. Aunt Hettie sits on the other side of me and joins in. We've all got tears in our eyes when we break away, and then we laugh.

Just then the door opens and Lesley walks into the room. "Oh, what a happy family," she says sarcastically.

My hackles rise immediately, but Miss Tina's voice echoes in my head. Lesley's given me a Cold Pricklie but I don't have to accept it or put it in my fuzzy bag, my heart. I can dodge it, and so I do.

"Hi Lesley," I say cheerfully, "how's it going?" A mental image of a yellow beanbag flying through the air pops into my mind.

She cusses at me and Mom stands up and sounds unusually stern. "You know the rules, Lesley. No cussing. That's a dollar off your allowance."

Lesley cusses at Mom.

"That's another dollar off your allowance. Keep going. The choice is yours," Mom spells it out. "I thought you were saving for those jeans you wanted."

Lesley opens her mouth to say something but then changes her mind and stomps up to her room.

My eyes are as wide as saucers and a giggle seeps out of me. "Mom! You were awesome," I say quietly so that Lesley can't hear me.

Mom grins and seems to stand taller. "I listened to what Miss Tina said, and guess what? Once I started to be strong with Lesley, it got easier. I just hit her where it hurts—money."

Suddenly my fears lessen. Mom has changed and I'm so proud of her.

Dad and Carol stop by later and it seems a bit weird all being in the same house, but the adults seem comfortable with it, so I stop worrying. Mom makes coffee.

"How does it feel to be home?" Carol asks me.

"It's good, although I'm going to miss Beach Haven and my new friends," I say.

"I bet you will," she replies. "It helped me so much that day we came. I've done a lot of thinking and I'm so sorry that I hurt you all. I know I'm not your mother, but I'm going to be your step-mother, and I hope we can be friends."

I glance at Mom to check out her reaction. She smiles and so I feel free to say what I think. "Of course," I say. "I feel a bit scared about how Millie is going to act with me. I mean, Lesley hasn't changed. She still hates me; I can see it on her face. I'm going to do everything Miss Tina's taught me, but if Millie and Lesley gang up to hurt me, I'm not going to put up with it. I need you to stand up to Millie. Will you?"

Carol suddenly looks uncomfortable. "I know what she did," she says in a small voice. "I feel ashamed. Her friend told me that she blackened her own eye on the side of a sink in the bathroom just to get you into trouble. I hate that, and I'm sorry it took me so long to see the truth. Trust me,

Maizy, I will stand up to Millie, and to Lesley. Do you believe me?" Then she smiles and surprises me by saying, "What did you hear me say?"

Instantly I feel warmth for her. I know that she has truly listened to Miss Tina and is using the active listening formula to check out if I understand what she's saying.

I smile and say, "I heard you say that you know what's been going on and you're going to stop it from happening again. Am I right?"

"Yes, you're absolutely right." Then Carol grins. "But Maizy, I don't think you have anything to worry about. Lesley and Millie had an argument days ago and now they hate each other, so I doubt that they'll be ganging up against anyone."

I don't say anything, as I don't believe that just because they've argued they'll stop being hateful, either alone or together.

Aunt Hettie breaks an awkward silence by offering everyone cookies, and I'm relieved. I know it's not going to be easy coping with the barrage of Cold Pricklies Lesley and Millie are likely to give me, but I'm going to try. I don't like either of them, but that doesn't matter. I still have a choice. I can give them Warm Fuzzies or Cold Pricklies, and I know that I want my heart, my fuzzy bag, to be full of Warm Fuzzies, so in a way, I have no choice. I will be nice to both of them and hope that they will eventually behave differently towards me. That's the bottom line.

Suddenly I'm tired and I want to go to my room. Everyone stands, and one by one they hug me. I head off to my bedroom and unpack my bag. I lay the shell necklace by the side of my bed, looking at it lovingly, as every memory from Beach Haven is refreshed in my memory. I lie on my bed, thinking. Already I miss everyone. I miss Velvet and her fierceness and wit, and I miss Lexi and her sense of freedom, but most of all I miss Marcus, who taught me what true intimacy is. A tear slides down my cheek as my longing for them is a raw wound, yet I tell myself that they're seconds away from me. My phone is by my bed and I have Beach Haven's number memorized. The thought comforts me and I drift off to sleep.

I'm awakened by someone knocking on my door. "Mom?" I call out, but the knocking continues. I get up and open the door. I take a sharp intake of breath. Ronan is standing in my bedroom doorway.

I feel suddenly awkward. I return to my bed and sit with my arms around my knees, defending myself. I don't know what I'm feeling. My head's spinning in confusion. Why's he here?

"Maizy," he starts to say, frowning and unsure of himself. "I'm sorry. I should have believed you. Mom and your dad have assured me that you didn't blacken Millie's eye. I feel terrible that I didn't believe you."

Hurt unfurls itself over me like the cold damp mist of betrayal. "Yes, you should have believed me. I loved you and I'd never have done anything to hurt you or your family. You really hurt me by believing that I could do such a thing."

He looks terrible, but with Miss Tina inside my head, I speak honestly, yet respectfully.

"I thought you knew me better than that," I say, trying to keep any whining out of my voice. I want to say it how it is without stepping onto the drama triangle. There's no way that I'm going to be a victim, and I don't want to be a persecutor or a rescuer. I just want to be real like I am with Marcus. I want nothing less than that, so I say what's on my mind. "It makes me sad to think that we were close and yet you didn't know me well enough to know that I'd never hurt your sister."

He hangs his head and apologizes over and over. I tell him that it's okay, because it really is. I know in this instance that I'm not in love with him anymore. Our relationship has changed, not only because we are forced to be brother and sister, but because he didn't have the faith in me to believe what I said. I tell him it's okay again and we hug.

"Let's just be friends, okay?" I say, and he nods. I grin at him. "After all, we're stuck with each other now."

He laughs tentatively and says, "Yes, I guess we are."

"I've never had a brother before, and I can't imagine having a nicer one than you," I say, meaning it.

"And you're better than any of my sisters," he replies, smiling at me, the tension slipping away from his face.

"You!" I poke him in the ribs.

"You, too!" he pokes me back, and we laugh, hugging again.

I feel weird. The pain I felt when Dad went off with Carol and I realized that Ronan and I could never be together was so awful. I felt destroyed by it. He was my first real boyfriend and I loved him so much, yet over the past few weeks at Beach Haven everything has changed. I've changed, and my thinking has changed. I look at him as he sits on the side of my bed awkwardly, and I feel love for him, but a different kind of love from the type I felt at Christmas. It's a different kind of love from the sort I feel for Marcus, who's my friend but not my boyfriend. I realize that life is complicated but exciting.

Mom shouts up the stairs saying that she's making us burgers, and Ronan goes downstairs while I change. As I walk down the stairs, I hear Mom talking to him, and I stop outside the kitchen door to listen.

"Ronan, I'm so sorry I was hateful to you when I told you to go, and I was mean about your mom,"

Mom says. "I was crazy at the time. I hope you can forgive me for the things I said. I didn't mean them. I think you're an amazing young man."

I hear Ronan reassure her that he doesn't feel any animosity towards her. Then I hear him confess to Mom how he messed up as badly as she had by believing Millie over me.

I walk into the kitchen and give Mom a hug. I'm proud of her for apologizing to Ronan for being so hateful to him when he came over in the new year to tell me that Dad and Carol had been seeing each other for ages and they were going to have a baby.

The burgers are ready and the smell of fried onions draws Lesley from her room. She walks through the kitchen ignoring us. I throw her a Warm Fuzzie. "Hey, are you going to eat with us?" I ask. She ignores me, but that's okay. My fuzzy bag is full of Warm Fuzzies, and I manage to deflect her Cold Pricklie. Actually she doesn't say anything—I guess she's too scared of being outwardly hateful in front of Mom in case she loses her allowance. It suits me.

When we've finished eating, Mom clears away the plates and the mess, and I'm astounded that she hasn't told me to do it. She seems so different and I feel like I'm going to burst with love for her.

Ronan says that he has to go, so I walk out with him to his car.

"Thank you so much for accepting my apology," he says, as he unlocks his car door.

I shrug. "You're welcome. Thanks for coming over."

I watch him settle into his seat and turn on the engine. He smiles at me, and says, "I'll see you soon, okay?"

"Okay. Come over any time, bro," I quip at him as he revs the engine.

"Will do."

I'm amazed that I don't feel sad or upset. I feel as if I've learned something monumental about life and love. I still love him but because he mistrusted me, I know that there's a limit to how intimate we can be. And as I think of the word "intimate" I smile to myself—I don't mean sex. I want the intimacy that Marcus and I shared, that had nothing to do with sex, and as I realize it, I know that I won't settle for anything less.

I look over at Mrs. White's house and remember her kindness towards me. Within the year I'll be going to college, thanks to her generosity. I'm going to work hard and make her proud of me. I think I'm going to be a therapist like Miss Tina so that I can help kids who feel as much pain as I used to. Yes, that feels right to me, and I'm sure Mrs. White would approve. I have just one year to go before leaving for college, and if Lesley and Millie continue to be mean, even though I will recognize the injustice of it all, I know I can cope with it and ignore them because I know what's inside my fuzzy bag.

I stand there filled with thoughts as Ronan's car screeches out of our drive and along the road. I feel warm and full of hope when suddenly I catch sight of something moving behind a bush from the corner of my eye. My heart races and I jump as a ball of black fur leaps into my arms. It's Sooty.

I remember how Sooty wouldn't have anything to do with me, and had run from me when she felt my distress that awful day after Ronan betrayed me and Mrs. White died. I thought she'd gone forever. She nestles next to my chest and purrs loudly. Maybe she senses the change in me. She licks my face and I kiss her nose. I hold her close and stroke her fur. "It's going to be all right," I whisper. "Trust me, it's going to be okay."

About the Author

Dr. Celia Banting earned her Ph.D. by studying suicide attempts in adolescents and developing a risk assessment tool to identify those young people who may be at risk of attempting suicide. She identified several risk factors which, when combined, could increase the likelihood of  an individual attempting suicide. Rather than write "how to" books or text books to help teenagers cope with the risk factors, Dr. Banting has incorporated therapeutic interventions into novels that adolescents will be able to identify with. These novels are designed to increase the adolescents' ability to take care of themselves, should they have minimal support in their families.

Dr. Banting's career has revolved around caring for children in a variety of settings in both the United Kingdom and the United States. She is dedicated to helping troubled children avoid the extreme act of suicide.

WIGHITA PRESS ORDER FORM

Book Title	Price	Qty.	Total

I Only Said I Had No Choice
ISBN 0-9786648-0-9 $14.99 x _____ $ _____
  Shane learns how to control his anger and make positive life
  choices; and he gains understanding about adult co-dependency.

I Only Said "Yes" So That They'd Like Me
ISBN 0-9786648-1-7 $14.99 x _____ $ _____
  Melody learns how to cope with being bullied by the in-crowd
  at school and explores the emotional consequences of casual
  sex. She raises her self-esteem and learns what true beauty is.

I Only Said I Couldn't Cope
ISBN 0-9786648-2-5 $14.99 x _____ $ _____
  Adam learns how to deal with grief and depression. He works
  through the grieving process and explores his perceptions of
  death and life.

I Only Said I Didn't Want You Because I Was Terrified
ISBN 0-9786648-3-3 $14.99 x _____ $ _____
  Hannah experiences peer pressure to drink alcohol. She learns
  about teenage pregnancy, birth, and caring for a new baby.
  Hannah faces the consequences of telling lies and learns how to
  repair broken trust.

I Only Said I Was Telling the Truth
ISBN 0-9786648-4-1 $14.99 x _____ $ _____
  Ruby embarks upon a journey to rid herself of the damaging
  emotional consequences of sexual abuse.

I Only Said I Could Handle It, But I Was Wrong
ISBN 9780978664855 $14.99 x _____ $ _____
  Simon embarks upon the most challenging journey of his
  life—to give up drugs, understand why he takes them and
  reclaim his life.

I Only Said It Didn't Hurt
ISBN 9780978664862 $14.99 x _____ $ _____
  Marsha cuts herself. As she learns how to cope with stress
  safely, she discovers a secret about herself that makes it
  impossible to ever cut again.

I Only Said I Wasn't Hungry
ISBN 9780978664879 $14.99 x _____ $ _____
  Ellie is bullied about her weight and sees food as her
  enemy. She learns to resist the voice of anorexia and explores
  the reasons for her poor self-image.

continued on reverse

WIGHITA PRESS ORDER FORM

Book Title	Price	Qty.	Total

I Only Said I Wanted to Kill Myself;
I Didn't Really Mean It
ISBN 9780978664886 $14.99   x _____ $ _____

    Kenny is angry and hates authority figures, but he forms
    a relationship with Miss Tina who teaches him how to
    get his needs met without acting up. He eventually understands
    why adults have to set rules.

I Only Said Leave Me Out of It
ISBN 9780978664893 $14.99   x _____ $ _____

    Maizy's parents divorce and she learns that, although
    it hurts when others are unkind or unjust, everyone has
    a choice as to how to respond. She finds a valued place
    in her new blended family.

Sub Total $_____

Sales Tax 7.5% ($1.13 per book) $_____

Shipping/handling $_____
1st book, $2.50; each add'l. book $1.00 / U.S. orders only.
(For orders outside the United States, contact Wighita Press.)

TOTAL DUE $_____

PLEASE PRINT ALL INFORMATION.

Customer name: _____

Mailing address: _____

City/State/Zip: _____

Phone Number(s): _____

E-mail address: _____

Make check or money order payable to Wighita Press and

mail order to: P.O. Box 30399, Little Rock, Arkansas 72260-0399

✦ ✦ ✦

Look for us on the web at: www.wighitapress.com

(501) 455-0905 or after office hours: (501) 952-1321